SHATTERED

SHATTERED

Every Crime Has A Victim

Lin Anderson

Ray Banks

Christopher Brookmyre

Karen Campbell

Gillian Galbraith

Alex Gray

Allan Guthrie

Stuart MacBride

GJ Moffat

Louise Welsh

First published in 2009 by Polygon,
an imprint of Birlinn Ltd,
West Newington House
10 Newington Road
Edinburgh
EH9 1QS
www.birlinn.co.uk
9 8 7 6 5 4 3 2 1

The publishers gratefully acknowledge the support of the
Russell Trust towards the publication of this volume.

ISBN 978 1 84697 127 3

British Library Cataloguing-in-Publication Data
A catalogue record for this book is available on request
from the British Library.

Typeset by Palimpsest Book Production Ltd,
Grangemouth, Stirlingshire, Scotland
Printed and bound by CPI Cox and Wyman, Reading, RG1 8EX

CONTENTS

PREFACE
The Rt Hon. Lord Ross
Former Lord Justice Clerk

During the years when I played a part in the criminal justice system in Scotland, I was, of course, aware that many people are adversely affected by crime. Indeed the effect a crime has had on a victim is something that a judge takes into account when sentencing an accused. However, in his Introduction to this volume, Ian Rankin makes the point that in crime novels, writers tend to concentrate on the criminal and to say little about the victim. Sadly, this is true also of the criminal justice system. The system quite rightly seeks to bring the perpetrators of crime to justice, but, at least until recently, inadequate attention has been paid to the interests and feelings of victims. Fortunately, that is now changing. It is now recognised that victims need to be given support in a variety of ways.

Broadly speaking, every crime has a victim. Physical or sexual assault may be the first to spring to mind, but many other crimes produce victims also – housebreaking, theft, fraud, road traffic offences, drug offences, and others too numerous to mention.

Organisations like Victim Support Scotland fulfil an important role in giving support and assistance to those injuriously affected by crime. This book has been produced in aid of Victim Support Scotland. It comprises a collection of short stories written by eminent Scottish crime writers who were invited to write a short story from the perspective of the victim. All the authors have generously donated their royalties to Victim Support Scotland. Each story describes how a victim has been affected, and serves to remind the reader of the different experiences of victims of crime. I hope the book will also inform the reader of some of the services that Victim Support Scotland provides.

I congratulate the authors on their excellent stories, and I commend the volume to all who enjoy reading this genre. To the latter I say – enjoy reading the book, and think of the sterling work that Victim Support Scotland does, and, if you can, give them your support in the future.

Donald M Ross
Edinburgh
August 2009

FORGOTTEN VOICES

Ian Rankin

The figure of the 'victim' has often been treated shabbily in literature. The crime novel in particular demands that there be a victim, just as it demands a criminal perpetrator, but often the various victims (usually of a murderer such as a serial killer) are little more than ciphers. We don't feel their fear and their pain because we readers are spectators after the fact. We arrive at the crime scene with the detective, and see only a body, representing a mystery to be solved. Or else we look through the killer's eyes as they stalk their unnamed prey. And if we *are* shown the hunt from the victim's point of view, there's little emotional pull on us because we know that the role they are playing in the story is minimal and that they will soon 'leave the stage' altogether, their voice unheard other than as a final blood-curdling scream or cry for help.

You see this, too, in horror films. How often have you watched on TV or in the cinema a character who is introduced only minutes before fleeing for her life (or, less often, *his* life) down shadowy alleys or badly lit corridors? We viewers know little or nothing about them, sometimes not even their name. They stumble and trip, clambering to their feet again, then run and run and eventually turn towards the horror behind them, only to find that it's no longer there . . . but that's only because it's *standing right next to them*, ready with a blade or an axe or a glove made of knives. When the credits roll at the end of the film, they may still lack any identity other than 'First Victim', 'Second Victim' and so on. Their role is to scare us and show us that nowhere is safe. Nemesis can never be avoided and everyone else in the story is likewise a potential victim.

The charity Victim Support Scotland decided to issue a challenge to some of the UK's pre-eminent crime writers – tell us a new story, this time from the victim's point of view. The authors responded with gusto, but also with nuanced consideration for the difficulties presented by the exercise. The crime novel is a cruel mistress, or even a straitjacket. There are conventions which a lot of us find hard to break. Many fans of the genre come to crime fiction for the pleasure of solving its puzzle – most usually formed as a 'whodunnit' with traps (in the shape of red herrings) laid along the way by the author. The best of these books probably belong to the so-called 'Golden Age', when authors such as Agatha Christie and Dorothy L Sayers played elegant games with their readers. Our fascination was with the detectives (Poirot or Marple or Lord Peter Wimsey) rather than the cunning and ruthless murderers, much less with their victims. Sympathy might lie with the poisoned Brigadier or strangled Countess, but they didn't engage us the way the other players did.

Fictional victims fared little better across the Atlantic. Famously, when Raymond Chandler was asked who killed the chauffeur in his novel *The Big Sleep*, he responded that he had no idea. The chauffeur was just a necessary addition to the body count. If he possessed a name, that was about as much as his creator required of him – it didn't matter why he had died or at whose hand. When 'Buffalo Bill' goes on his killing spree in Thomas Harris's *The Silence of the Lambs*, his victims are a means to an end – for killer and author both. It's FBI trainee Clarice Starling and psychopath Hannibal Lecter we're really interested in. After finishing the book, most of us will readily forget the names of the victims we've encountered fleetingly along the way.

I remember my literary agent in the USA telling me that my books would sell more copies there if I moved the murder to the opening page of the story. Up until then, sometimes nobody died in my books until page 100, but American readers liked to be plunged into the intrigue, rather than led slowly towards it. This gives the victim even less time to impinge upon the consciousness (and conscience) of the reader. Again, their only requirement is that they suffer and then cease to exist.

Does this matter? Well, yes, actually it does. In recent years crime fiction (in the UK and elsewhere) has come out of the library or the billiard-room and on to the streets and housing schemes most of us recognise. In other words, there's a new sense of realism and veracity. Crime writers want to tell the truth about the world we all live in. Reading a book may be a form of escapism, but that doesn't mean readers want to be wrapped in cotton wool, and writers have responded by tackling serious subject matter and asking big moral questions. Racism, bullying, abuse and sectarianism can all be tackled in the contemporary crime story. Corporate greed and political corruption can be challenged and vilified. Readers will be asked, what makes us do bad things? What might turn *you* into a killer or a vigilante? What sort of mess is society in, and is there anything we can do about it? But crime writers must also pay attention to the victims in all these stories. They can't just be cardboard cut-outs from central casting. We have to put flesh and blood on them and explore their inner lives, showing their hopes as well as their fears, giving them life as well as death.

Scotland is fortunate to be able to boast some of the finest writers in the world. In this book, you'll find compelling and considered stories from the best practitioners around. You'll also find the figure of the victim brought centre stage, where, really, he or she belonged all along.

Ian Rankin
Edinburgh
August 2009

DADDY'S GIRL
Karen Campbell

'Mammy?'

Two sharp eyes from tangled-hedge curls.

'What, honey?' She was stirring a pot of something, one eye on the telly that strummed a daily diet of cartoons through their tidy bedsit.

'Mammy. Who's ma daddy?'

Irene added some salt. With each grain that sprinkled, an answer fell too. She watched salt dissolve as it struck hot liquid, each possibility melting. Since before Jess could talk, this question had hung, thick as the hair above her quizzical brows. Irene saw her look at men pushing prams; men playing chase; men giving piggybacks. But she'd never yet asked – where's mine?

'Your daddy had to go away, pet.'

'I know *that*, Mammy,' she tutted imperiously. 'But who is he?'

Unsure of which child development expert to follow, Irene tended to pick and mix – a bit of Stoppard here, some Dr Spock there, some touchy-feely Sheila Kitzinger on occasion (though she drew the line at frying up her own placenta). And, when all else failed, a good skelp on the bahookie. But when it came to answering the steady torrent of questions her daughter unleashed each day, Irene was constant – if they're old enough to ask, they're old enough to know. So it was that Jess was the only child in Primary One to point out Thomas Mearns didn't have a winky – he had a *penis*. And, not only could she spell and write her name before she started school, Jess also had a fair grasp of the solar system, and, on a fine clear night, could point out 'Big Ted' and 'Wee Ted' twinkling in the heavens. All because she asked.

'Well, you know,' said Irene, turning the pot handle inwards and coming over to sit by her on the couch, 'some wee boys and girls don't have daddies.'

'How no'?'

Irene turned the sound down on *The Powerpuff Girls*.

'Well, they maybe didn't love the mummy anymore. Or, maybe they died. Or, maybe they didn't know they had a wee baby.'

'How no'?'

This was the pattern of all their Q&A sessions. Jess would chew a bit, digest a bit, then take another bite. Of course, all mothers know their child is brilliant (and beautiful), but the ferocity of Jess's intelligence could scare Irene. Insistently tugging her further down a path she didn't want to go. Deeper and deeper, in they would lurch, until Jess was either satisfied or bored. Irene felt sometimes she couldn't keep up. Once, fighting the urge to scream 'Just because!', Irene had said, 'Why do you need to keep asking all these questions, Jess?'

Jess had looked at her and replied, 'Because I'm only little, Mammy. And I need to know.'

Funny then, that she'd never asked this most obvious of questions. This not-having that Irene worked so hard at to ignore. Like an old auntie stinking faintly of wee, nobody mentioned it, though the smell pervaded everything.

'Why do you want to know?'

Jess shifted a little, tucking her stocky legs beneath her. ''Cause Andrea says I was made in a lavaritory.' She spoke quietly.

'A what?'

'A lavaritory. She says if I don't have a daddy I must of got made in a wee tube by doctors.'

'Och, pet,' Irene hugged her daughter into her, 'She means a laboratory, and, no, you weren't made there. But, yes, some doctors help mummies and daddies that can't have their own babies by, well, by sort of mixing it up in a tube thing.'

'You mean the egg and the seed, Mammy,' said Jess solemnly.

'That's right.'

'Then do they put it back in the mummy's tummy?'

'Yes, they do.'

Jess nodded.

'But that didn't happen to me?'

'No, darling, it didn't.'

'Well . . .'

'Oh, look Jess – it's *Pet Rescue* on the other side. I wonder if that wee kitten got better. Mind the one that was knocked down last week?'

Instantly, Jess's eyes were on the screen. 'Oh, the wee soul. Look Mammy – it's in a cage.'

Irene stood up. 'It's all right. That's it in the hospital. It'll be fine now. You just watch and make sure, okay?'

The child was transfixed. They weren't allowed pets in the bedsit. Even so, or perhaps because, Jess loved animals – including the spiders Irene couldn't bear. Jess would squat on the floor, hold out her chubby hand, and let the things walk right on, with their big, hairy, clatty legs. Then, very gently, she'd carry the spider or the slater or whatever she'd found to the window and put it on the ledge.

'Right, I'm going to put the tea out, then it's bathtime for you, young lady.'

Jess nodded, eyes intent on the comatose cat.

Irene went back to the two rings and basin that were allegedly a kitchen, and dished out mince and potatoes for two. After tea, they played a game. It was one of Jess's favourites, where you each draw a head, then fold the page over and pass it on. The next person draws a body without seeing the head, then the next draws legs and feet. They called it the baw-heid game. It didn't really work with two, but they always made sure none of the bits matched up, so it was funnier when the paper got unfolded at the end. You might have a monkey's head with a snowman's body and a ballet dancer's legs. But it would have been better with more people drawing.

Once she got Jess down, Irene cleared the tiny table and switched on the lamp. All the other lights were off so the child could get to sleep, and, often, Irene would join her. There was nowhere comfy to sit once the couch was folded down. Tonight, however, her essay was late. She'd been granted a grudging extension already, and there was no way her tutor would stretch his sympathy further. And why should he?

About four in the morning, Irene finally switched off the light and climbed in beside her daughter. The shivering had begun to affect her writing. The deadline was 11 a.m., the essay virtually done. If they got up early tomorrow, she could take Jess into uni with her, type it up on one of the computers in the library. They'd need to be in by eight. There was a crèche there, which she was allowed to use in the holidays. Irene was sure if she asked nicely, Linda the nursery lady would sit Jess down with a wee bit toast and some crayons. It would only be for an hour or two. It would mean her missing a morning of school, but she could say they had the dentist's or something.

Irene was tired beyond feeling, yet her brain would not give her peace. Day or night, relentless, constant fretting – who'd pick the wee one up from school on Wednesday? How could she afford the electricity this week? Why had Jess, Jess who relished bugs, suddenly decided her favourite spaghetti 'was evil worms' and not to be endured? When was Irene going to study for her finals?

Why was she on her own?

See, if her mum or dad had helped out, just now and then, that would have made such a difference, to their own lives too – let them see what they were missing. When she said she was going to have the baby, they went mental. Called her for everything. Was she insane? Did she know what this would do to her life, her future? What would the neighbours say? How could they possibly cope? Then, when she said not only was she going to have it, she was going to keep it, they just freaked. Her father threw her out of the house. Her own dad, who used to carry her on his shoulders and make the best eggy soldiers in the world, had grabbed her by the elbow, wrenched open the door, and shoved her into the rain. Irene standing in the street, with her hair all wet, shouting 'Don't, Daddy, don't.' Her mum had run after her, took her to her Auntie Belle's 'until things calmed down a bit'. Things never calmed down enough. The swell of her father's silence matched the hardening of Irene's intent. She had been so raw, and now the scar tissue was stretching, fusing. Tough enough to leave Auntie Belle's. No one knew where she had gone, and, as always, they were in the right. So. Well then. They had washed their hands of her and the child, and that was it.

Looking at Jess, wee thumb searching for sleep-pursed lips, Irene wondered at it all. Wondered at a mother that could let her daughter down. Who did not feel the furious need to protect and succour, a need so strong that you had no choice. She kissed her daughter on the forehead, and fell asleep at last.

In the morning, the usual rush and guddle. Irene tried to make Jess eat porridge, she really did. But Coco Pops were so much quicker. Even then, she spoon fed her, shovelling them in as Jess gawped at Pokemon. At the weekend, they'd have porridge. Porridge and French toast. And they'd have it in bed. Then her friend Shirley would take her to McDonald's, and wouldn't that be fun? No, Mammy wasn't coming. She was going to do some studying.

'Is that for how you can get your new job, Mammy?'

'Yes, honey, that's right. Now, hurry up and get your coat on.'

'And then will we get our nice new house-with-a-garden?'

'Hopefully, yes. Are you all done with your breakfast?'

'Yes. And, Mammy?'

'What, darling? Come on now, button yourself up. It's cold out.' Irene grabbed her notes from the table, stuck them in a poly bag.

'When we get a garden, can I get a cat?'

'We'll see. Now, come on, or we'll miss the bus.'

They had to run, Jess flapping her arms like an angry sparrow. 'Wait, Mister Bus Man. Wait the now!'

Obligingly, he did as he was told.

'That's a fine pair of lungs you've got on you there, hen,' he said, taking their money.

'Thank you,' said Jess politely, looking down at her chest.

There was only one seat left, so Irene took Jess on her knee.

'Listen, pet, I've a wee secret,' she whispered in her ear.

'What?' yawned Jess. It was an hour before their usual bus journey, but Jess couldn't do time yet. Well, she'd never asked.

She was playing with Irene's hair, leaning back against her mother's stomach, reaching up casually behind to twirl it through her fingers. As if Irene was an extension of herself.

'See this morning, would you mind if you missed a wee bit school? It's just, Mammy has to finish her work at the uni. If you sit nice and quiet with Linda, I'll get us some sweeties on the way home.'

'Okay, Mammy.' Then, after a moment, 'Will I still get a play piece, too?'

'Yes, Linda'll give you something. But, mind how I said it was a secret, well,' she leant in close to Jess's ear, 'kid on to your teacher you were at the dentist's, okay?'

'Why?'

'Mammy could get into trouble.'

'How?' Jess looked round now, surprised.

''Cause I'm supposed to make sure you go to school.'

'But we're going to your school instead, aren't we?'

'Yes, we are.'

Jess settled back on her mother's lap, moulding into her once more. Irene kissed the top of her head.

'You're a clever girl.'

'Andrea's daddy takes her to school.'

She knew it was coming. Still snug up against her daughter's head. Nuzzling her hair, drowning in the sweet sleep smell on her baby's neck. She remembered the smell more than anything. She knew it was coming. They had dragged her into the toilets in the park. Stinking of men and urine, they'd held her on the floor. Cold white-grey tiles pressing on her face. Or she had pressed her face on them, trying to push herself through the unyielding, filthy floor, to make herself not there. There were three of them. At least. Fat thumbs in her mouth. Yellow pus nicotine tattoo. Filthy fingernails clawing cigarette stench. Choking while they laughed. Oh God, Oh God, Oh God.

Afterwards, when they'd left her bleeding on the piss and shit swimming floor, the urinal had flushed. Did it automatically, apparently. She'd watched her blood swirl down, jigging as it went. It seemed too sprightly a movement; had shocked her. She'd pulled herself to her feet and run, slipping on wet tiles. Screaming with the voice that had left her alone and unprotected all the time she had needed it. Screaming and screaming, naked past the children on the swings. Screaming and screaming past the boys playing five-a-sides. Screaming and screaming past the broken glass that embedded itself with vicious teeth in her soft skin. Until someone had grabbed her, made her stop. They'd wrapped her in a coat and phoned the police. There, it smelled of Dettol and cooked cabbage. When they'd finished swabbing, her mum arrived to take her home. Talcum powder and furniture polish, and brittle, accusing not-looks.

She knew it was coming.

'Mammy – who *is* my daddy?'

Irene felt the old woman across the aisle listening. She felt the whole world listening, listening to her run naked through dog crap with bloody feet. Forcing out words from her screaming lungs.

'You're daddy was a very special man, Jess. He loved you very much.'

'Where is he, but?'

'He had to go away.'

'Where?'

Salt in the pot. She could taste it in her mouth. 'He had to go to Heaven.'

'To see God?'

Voice in her hair, burning more tears back. 'Aye, that's right.'

'But he still loves me?'

Whisper it. 'Yes.'

Jess waited. Sucked a while on Irene's hair. 'So, why did God do that, Mammy?'

'I don't know, pet. Just because.'

RUN, RABBIT, RUN
Ray Banks

Terry Davies started on the beers around kick-off, and continued through final whistle until his knees felt loose. Now he held on to a table, a fresh pint in his free hand, nodding as Marto gave him the lad's name.

Billy Lewis.

Didn't ring any bells; could've been anyone. But the way Marto told it, nobody called the lad Billy, anyway: to him and the blokes Marto had been talking to, the lad's name was Rabbit, and Rabbit was a smackhead on licence with priors coming out his arse. It was juvenile odds and sods that put him in the big boys' nick, and Marto wanted to make it clear that this wasn't Keyser fucking Söze they were dealing with here.

'Lad's done some shite – breaking and entering you know about. Handling stolen goods. Got done for possession with intent, and that's the most serious, like. But I don't want you thinking he's owt worth getting scared about.'

'I'm not scared.'

'Nah, I know you're not scared,' shouted Marto against the noise of the pub. 'I didn't mean it like that. All I'm saying, you want to do something –'

Terry waved his hand, looked behind Marto at the people lining the far wall, but didn't really see any of them. 'I haven't made a decision yet.'

'You were the one wanted us to keep an ear out.'

'I know. I appreciate it.'

'Not like I give a fuck what you do, like. I'm not putting any pressure on or nowt.'

'I know you're not, man.' Terry smiled, but it didn't seem to stay on his face. 'I'm just saying that I want to have a think about it.'

Marto held up one hand. 'Nae bother, son. You do that, take all the time you need.' He leaned in, trying to keep his voice down, but the gist was clear: 'But he's not fuckin' hard, if that's what's worrying you. Streak of piss, stiff breeze'd knock him on his arse.'

'He's a runner,' said Terry.

'How'd you know that?'

'Rabbit.'

'Wey aye, that's why. I never thought.'

Terry tapped a temple. 'Fuckin' brains, me.'

'So y'are.' Marto gulped back some of his beer, showed his teeth and bucked his head as he belched. 'How, tell you, see if it was me? And he'd done to me what he did to you?' He pulled a sick face. 'I'd chin the cunt into the middle of next week.'

'I know you would.'

'But that's me.'

'Aye, that's you.'

'I'm fuckin' emotional.' One last drink to punctuate, then: 'All I'm saying is, you want to find him, the lad's easy fuckin' found.'

'That right?'

'Has to go to the Addictions to give a sample, else he's back in the nick. Big car park outside the place, you could wait there, nobody'd bat a fuckin' eye.'

Terry rolled his tongue around the inside of his mouth. He was warm, felt sweaty. 'What does he look like?'

'Like a smackhead streak of piss,' said Marto. 'Shaved head, got this tattoo of a Jew star on the side of his neck.'

Terry grimaced. 'His neck?'

'That don't make him hard. He's soft as clarts, everyone says.'

'Everyone?'

Marto grinned, held up his empty pint glass. 'How, you want all the gen, you're gonna have to get another round in.'

They stepped out of the pub and leaned against the wall to focus. Their breath misted in front of their faces.

'You need any help . . . on it,' said Marto.

'Nah.'

'You'll think?'

'Aye.'

'Wey, then. Take care.'

Terry clapped him on the shoulder, and Marto lumbered off down the road. Terry watched him go, the street lights throwing a sick orange glow over everything. Marto walked with his legs going in opposite directions, and Terry knew he'd be the same once he pushed away from the wall.

Promised he'd think about it, but there wasn't a lot to think about. What Marto told him, if Terry didn't do it, someone else would. This lad Rabbit owed cash all over the fucking shop, pissed off the kind of villains who wouldn't think twice about battering fuck out of a junkie, even if it was just for giggles and small change.

He launched himself off the wall and dug both hands into his jacket pockets, striding forward as straight as he could. He wanted a tab, but didn't think he'd be able to smoke and walk at the same time, so he kept concentrating on the pavement, watching his feet, until he got home. There he fished around for his keys, scratched at the paint-work for a good minute before he realised they'd had to change the locks.

His missus came to the door, one fist keeping her dressing gown closed, her other hand trembling with something other than the cold. She opened up on the chain first and regarded him with blank eyes. Then she unlocked the door, left it ajar and went back to the lounge.

She hadn't been sleeping, which meant Terry hadn't been sleeping, either. Wide awake and stiff as a board at the slightest noise, convinced that it was happening again, and she wouldn't take anything for it, wouldn't relax. When he suggested medication, it was as if he'd suggested she take cyanide instead of Nytol. So he stopped suggesting it, and tried to find other options.

'You're late.' She was perched on the edge of the settee, watching the telly, some cheap drama about cops and killers. 'You stink an' all.'

'I know.' He sat on the settee next to her, watched a couple of cops banter on for a bit. 'I saw Marto.'

'What'd he say?'

'He got us a name.'

She nodded, a sharp little movement. 'That all?'

'No.'

'Okay.'

He glanced across at her. In the flickering light of the telly, she looked older than she was, her eyes hollow and deep wrinkles slashing at the edges of her perpetually pinched mouth. She looked at her hands, knotted together in her lap, and swallowed. 'So what you going to do?'

He looked back at the telly. The cops were at a crime scene, a body face down in the middle of the floor, and they were talking about the pretty patterns the blood had made when it sprayed up the wall. Terry put one hand over hers and squeezed. 'I'm going to sort it,' he said.

On Monday morning, nice and early, he phoned in sick. Said he had a bug; he'd been up all night with the sickness and diarrhoea; didn't think he'd be in for a couple of days at least. There weren't many questions after that. People he worked for, they didn't want to know the gory details, and with Terry's clean sick record, he reckoned they probably owed it to him anyway. He drove to Freehold Street, where he parked a good way back from the entrance to the Addictions place and got settled in for the day.

By nine o'clock, the place was open. He watched them come and go, got to know the clients by the way they looked. A couple with a bairn in a pushchair – the girl with a fat arse and telling the stocky bloke that she'd seen these lush tops in Primark, and as soon as she got her dole, that'd be her. An old man with a face like a burst balloon who looked more like an alkie than a smackhead, shambling pigeon-toed and tired, and trailing a smell that could strip paint. Two lads on bikes, swinging around the car park, waiting on a third, older lad, who came out of the Addictions smiling yellow and black, announcing that his piss test was done.

The afternoon came, and Terry put on the radio, confident that nobody had seen him. Classical music filled the car. Sort of thing he listened to when he had the Cavalier to himself, none of your avant-garde stuff, just the standards. Relaxation music.

Terry took a drink of water. Just a sip to wet his mouth. Last thing he needed was to be bursting for a piss when Rabbit showed his face. He put the cap on the bottle, and the bottle on the dash, and he swallowed against a quickly drying throat. Got to thinking about what he had to do, like if he was the kind of bloke to go out and bray a lad, even if he had a fucking good reason. He hadn't been in a fight since he was a kid, and even then it'd been mostly just him defending himself against bigger lads. Marto – oh aye, Marto – now he was the kind of bloke who could be the full-on radge merchant, no sweat, but Terry wasn't sure about himself. Wasn't that he didn't have the bottle – he had plenty of that; enough to spare, even – but it wasn't something he'd done before, and there was a loud part of him that was worried he'd freeze.

He looked at the rounders bat. He'd taken it from the garage, where it had sat in the summer box with the swing-ball. Kids wouldn't miss it, and he'd replace it before the holidays. Couldn't have his bairns playing rounders with a bloodstained bat. Just like he couldn't have his missus staying up all night every night, going steadily mental to *ITV Nightscreen*. It wasn't right.

Terry looked up, blinked against the sunshine. The radio was playing Wagner, that tune that reminded him of the old Bugs Bunny cartoon where Elmer Fudd runs around in a big Viking helmet.

'Kill da wabbit' and all that.

He smiled, moving away from the light. Shielded his eyes and saw a figure heading towards the Addictions. He was a long lad, a wide walk on him, and a thin layer of stubble covered his head. Terry shifted in his seat, tried to get a better look.

Rabbit. Maybe. Could've been. He couldn't really tell at this distance.

Terry reached for the bat.

The lad turned a little, and then Terry saw it, the tattoo, the one Marto had called a Jew star. It was large and spindly and blue, and it covered the left side of Rabbit's neck from shoulder to just under the ear. Couldn't miss it.

And then he was gone, ducked inside the Addictions place.

Terry took another swig of water, a large one. No longer worried about needing a piss. This would be over soon enough. He felt the weight of the rounders bat and breathed through his nose. His heart threw itself against the inside of his ribcage, and he noticed a tremor in his arms. He didn't know how long Rabbit was going to be in there, but he needed to get himself sorted for when the lad came out. He wouldn't get many chances like this, not if the lad was a runner.

So he focused on the entrance. Pictured the lad going up the stairs to reception, taking a seat. If he was on licence, he was probably doing a piss test, and it didn't take very long to drop off a sample. Terry watched a couple of blokes, same loose limbs as the rest of the smackheads who'd been in there this morning, and his gut lurched. He hadn't thought about witnesses, had it all planned different.

The two blokes stopped by the entrance, their backs to the door. One of them, a gadgie with long black hair, lit a tab and passed the pack to his mate, who had the strong but fattish build of a doorman.

Fuck it, it didn't matter if there were people around or not.

Three minutes by the clock in the dash, and Rabbit stepped out of the Addictions. Terry pushed out of the car in one movement, picking up the bat as he went. Kept his head down, thinking it was now or never, thinking about the missus, thinking about the kids, thinking about the broken conservatory window and the stolen jewellery, PS3 and DVDs. Thinking about that junkie fuckin' scum deserving everything he gets, and getting his blood up so Terry could do this, go back to his missus and tell her everything was okay, everything was sorted, that she could sleep tonight safe in the knowledge that the man who'd violated their home was twitching in the gutter outside the Substance Abuse Team office –

He heard a scream, and a car alarm went off.

'Howeh, the fuckin' money, Rabbit, eh? You fuckin' holding or what?'

Terry looked up. Saw the doorman with Rabbit thrown up onto the bonnet of an old-style Merc, and Rabbit was trying to yell for help through the blood in his mouth. The bloke with the long black hair had something in his hand, something wicked sharp that caught the light and flashed it across the tarmac, while the doorman went to work on Rabbit's gut.

Terry ran towards them. Couldn't help himself. He yelled at them, the words scrambling out of his mouth before he had a chance to stop and think. 'Fuck off, the pair of youse, he's *mine*.'

The doorman turned his head, the other bloke stepping back. Both glanced at the bat in Terry's hand, then at the look in his eyes. Terry kept going, couldn't stop now. The doorman laughed and let Rabbit slide off the bonnet, then the pair of them started backing off.

'Fuckin' hell, Rabbit, you're popular the day, aren't you?' The bloke with the hair grinned at Terry. 'You're welcome to sloppy seconds, mate.'

Terry raised the bat, and the two men moved a little quicker. The car alarm still shrieked, made his head hurt.

Rabbit lay in a pile on the tarmac. Blood all over his face. Already beaten. There was a gash in his side, and his T-shirt was soaked red, but he was still breathing. Terry looked up at the Addictions building – people in the windows, looking back at him and Rabbit.

His arms buzzed with adrenaline, and he was aware he was breathing through his teeth.

Rabbit looked up. 'Thanks, man.'

Terry felt the energy drain from him, and he lowered the bat. His brain screamed at him to use it, but his body had other ideas. He looked around him, and he felt like crying. He gripped the bat in both hands like handlebars, then threw it onto the tarmac. It clattered and rolled towards the Merc. Rabbit watched it, then looked back up at Terry. 'I know you?'

Terry heard sirens through the wail of the car alarm. Probably an ambulance, probably for Rabbit, and probably called by the Addictions staff who were watching him right now.

'Nah,' he said. 'You don't know me, kidda.'

And he turned back to the car where he slept like a baby for the first time in weeks.

BYE, BYE, BABY
Allan Guthrie

Banging at the door again. It's the police.

They're going to tell me my son's dead, I know it.

While they were gone, I've emptied the drinks cabinet, downed most of what I can find. Vodka, whisky, sherry. Couldn't face the crème de menthe.

Me and alcohol. Shouldn't have the stomach for each other. I'm still sober enough to appreciate the irony of that.

More banging.

Maybe they'll tell me to calm down again. Like that'll help. Your child goes missing, you don't calm down.

And do they care anyway? No, they left me here on my own while they hightailed it to talk to the teachers. As if those bastards were ever going to be of any help. And Lyle? Even less.

Jesus, I could use another drink. Only let booze back into the house a couple of years ago. I did bloody good, all right?

I think I said that, though. To the police. Not about the alcohol. About the teachers. About them being liars. Did I say that? I don't know what I said. Not got Bruce to remind me, have I? He's gone. Gone, sweet Jesus.

That pounding again. My pulse throbbing in time with it. They're not going to go away. They know I'm at home.

'Mrs Wilson?'

That'll be me. I should answer. But my legs won't move. If the police tell me he's dead, I don't know what I'll do.

★

A couple of hours earlier, the two officers were sitting in my living room. A male and a female, can't remember their names. I'm not so good with names these days. I hadn't offered them tea like I was supposed to. Maybe that was rude. But a cup of tea was neither here nor there, surely.

'In your own time,' the policewoman said. 'What happened?'

'I went to pick up Bruce from school.' I looked at them, one after the other. The woman rested the end of her pen against her chin, her mouth slightly open. Her male colleague scratched his cheek. He looked crumpled, from his face to his shoes. I kept it simple for them. 'He wasn't there.'

'You usually pick him up where, exactly?'

'No,' I said, shaking my head.

'No?'

I kept shaking my head, aware that I must look daft. 'Not "usually",' I said. 'Always. I always pick him up outside the school gates. I'm always there when the bell rings.'

'And he wasn't there today?'

'That's right.'

'He wasn't in his classroom?'

Give me strength. I didn't even bother answering that one.

'Maybe one of the other parents . . . ?'

I was shaking my head again, so the policewoman stopped talking, wrote something in her notebook.

After a while, she said, 'How can you be so sure?'

'I stay out of their business. They stay out of mine.'

Caught a look between the officers, as if I'd said something significant. Maybe I had. Nobody wanted to hear about tragedy. People want to get on with their lives and tragedy holds you up. Even someone else's tragedy can hold you up. It can infect you like some kind of wasting disease. Surprised no one's asked me to wear a bell round my neck so they can hear me coming.

Didn't want to think about bells. Could still hear the school bell ringing.

'What about the boy's father?'

Of course, they didn't know. Course they didn't. Talking about it didn't hurt quite so much now. I'd learned over the years how best to handle it.

'John's dead,' I said. Caught another look between them, this time with a touch more sympathy in it. 'Car crash,' I continued. 'Got ploughed into head-on by a drunk driver. Bastard took a corner on the wrong side of the road.' These days I didn't even bother adding that he'd survived. 'Killed John.' Sometimes I think I don't blame anybody, but I'm not fooling myself. I blame everybody.

'I'm very sorry to hear that.' Strangely enough, it was the bloke who replied. He pressed his thumb into the crease above his lip as if it helped him to think. When his hand moved away, I noticed his scar. Maybe he'd fallen and punched a hole through the skin with a tooth when he was a boy. It was the sort of thing kids did, wasn't it?

'How old was your son at the time?' he asked.

'It happened seven years ago in March,' I told him. 'Bruce was just a baby. Eight months old.'

Look at me! Dry eyes. That's progress.

The police officers didn't know what to say. They both cleared their throats. I almost felt sorry for them.

Eventually, the male officer said, 'Do you have a photo of Bruce, Mrs Wilson?'

'Bruce is camera shy.'

'It doesn't have to be a good photo. Anything will do. Just so we have a likeness.'

I said, slower this time, 'Bruce is camera shy,' and waited for the next question. But they liked this one.

'You don't have *any* photos?' the bloke asked again.

'He doesn't fucking like having his photo taken,' I said, probably a little too sharply judging by their wide-eyed response. I said it again, softer, without swearing, eyes downcast like a good fucking girl.

'What about a school photograph?'

'What is it you don't get?' I said, getting to my feet and banging my shins against the coffee table. I used the pain to help me focus. 'I won't put Bruce through any kind of ordeal. I won't do that. He's suffered enough, losing his father. Can you imagine what that's like? I know he's too young to understand, but the older he gets, the more it shows and he acts out and . . . and I let him, I suppose. Maybe I spoil him a bit. But he hurts. I know. I feel it.' And now I was crying and angry with myself for losing control. I shook the tears away. 'My boyfriend says Bruce is damaging our relationship. Can you believe that? Blaming my baby?'

'What's your boyfriend's name?'

'I should have said ex-boyfriend,' I said. 'Lyle. I got fed up with his jealousy. I finished with him about a week ago. Told him to leave us alone. And that's what he's done.'

'Lyle who?'

'Whittaker. Lyle Whittaker.'

'Do you have his address?'

I gave it to them. The female officer wrote it down in her notebook.

'I'm sorry to have to ask this,' her colleague said, 'but did your relationship with Mr Whittaker end amicably?'

I shrugged. 'He called me a mad bitch. But he didn't throw any punches. Is that amicable?'

'Might Mr Whittaker have picked up Bruce from school?'

'Lyle wouldn't dream of it.'

'I think we should talk to him anyway.'

'Whatever you think.'

We sat for a bit, staring at each other. Then the woman said, 'Could we see Bruce's room?'

'Why not.' I got to my feet, led them down the hallway and up the stairs. I swung Bruce's bedroom door open and stepped inside.

They followed me in, started to look around. I half expected them to make a note of the titles of all the books in his bookcase, list all the games stacked in the corner, the toys in their boxes. I could do it blindfold.

'No TV?' the male officer asked.

'I don't like him watching too much TV.'

'Computer?'

'He's not old enough to be interested.'

'Really? My two were into computers from before they could speak.'

'You have two boys?'

'Yeah. Older one just had his thirteenth birthday. His brother's ten.'

I was about to ask their names when the female officer asked, 'Have you tidied up in here?'

'No need. Bruce is a neat little boy.'

'Very,' she said. 'Noticed anything missing? Clothes, maybe? Money?'

'Money?' I said.

'I just wondered,' she said. 'Kids sometimes have a bit of cash stashed away.'

'Not Bruce,' I said. 'He doesn't need money.'

She looked at me again, waiting for something. 'Clothes?' she said. 'Any clothes missing?'

I shook my head.

'Can you take a look, please, just to make sure?'

Sweet Jesus. I pulled out the drawers, pretended to scan through the wardrobe. A couple of minutes later, I said, 'Everything's here. Apart from what he's wearing.'

'Let's go over that once again,' she said.

I told them he was wearing his school uniform, and described it, and mentioned the Hearts scarf he liked, which he wasn't allowed to wear in class. He always took it off outside the school gates and stuffed it in his schoolbag.

The male officer said, 'And there's really not a single photo of him?'

If I wasn't such a nice person I'd have leapt across the room and choked him. Instead, I looked into his narrow blue eyes and said, 'John was the positive one.'

The officer looked puzzled for just a second.

Fuck it, I wanted to make him feel bad. I wanted some company.

'Bruce's dad,' I said, and then added, 'My husband. Remember?'

The poor bloke winced and nodded and said, 'Yes, yes,' and mumbled, 'John, of course.'

I was a bitter, twisted bitch.

But I was paying for it.

Memories faded and vanished. It was only a question of when.

'You know what it's like not being able to say sorry?' I said. I felt my fists clench. 'We'd argued, me and John. Just before . . . It was a silly thing, didn't know it would become important. He hadn't shaved for a couple of days. I asked him if he was growing a beard. He was already stressed out, rough day at work. I didn't realise how much until he told me to shut up. Told me to stop nagging him. That was the day before the accident. And I never apologised to him, and now I can't tell him I'm sorry. Can't tell him that he looked just fine.' I couldn't picture his face any longer, couldn't see the offending stubble. 'I was a total fucking idiot! I've lost John. I can't lose Bruce too.'

'I think you should sit down,' the female officer said. 'Calm yourself. And don't jump to conclusions.'

'Yeah,' I said. 'Okay.'

I was out of breath. I'd been walking up and down, pumping my fists. I needed a drink.

So here they are back from talking to the teachers, speaking to Lyle. If I didn't know better I'd say from the sound of the banging at the door that they're annoyed. Maybe Lyle said something bad about me. And no doubt the teachers were no help. Nothing new there. Should have warned the police before they left. The school doesn't like me.

The banging. Annoyed banging. Not urgent.

Annoyed, yes.

It'll be okay.

I get my legs moving, stumble to the door, and when I open it, the police officers stare at me like something terrible's happened.

God, let Bruce be okay.

In a voice that sounds more formal than earlier, the male officer says, 'Can we come in?'

I lead them back to the sitting room, walking carefully so they don't spot I've been drinking. I want to ask them what's happened to Bruce but I'm afraid of the answer. I offer them tea, remembering my manners. No, that's not true, I'm trying to postpone what they're about to tell me.

But they don't want tea. Or coffee. And then I notice the empty bottles lying around and start to clear them away. Then I realise all I'm doing is drawing attention to them, so I just leave them where they are. Hidden in plain sight.

Although they're not hidden at all.

Everything's out in the open now.

The officers are looking at each other. Seems as if they're egging each other on to say something but neither of them has the courage.

I hear myself say, 'How did you get on?'

'To tell the truth, it was a bit of an eye-opener,' the male officer says.

For a moment, I'm thinking this is a good thing, but then I see his face and realise it's not.

'We spoke to Mrs Lennox, the headmistress.'

I nod.

'And Bruce's teacher, Mrs Carruthers.'

I nod again.

He looks as if he wants to say more, but can't.

His colleague takes over. 'They told us about the accident, Clare.'

Oh, God. Oh, God, no.

'An accident?' I whisper. 'Bruce has been in an accident?' I shouldn't have answered the door.

'They told us how you and John and Bruce were in the car that night.'

'Yes.' Yes, we were. But I wonder what that has to do with Bruce being missing.

'Your ex-boyfriend, Mr Whittaker . . . Lyle . . . he told us too. How John . . . how John died on impact.'

Died on impact. Sounds so much better than 'crushed to death'.

'They told us how you suffered terrible injuries and almost died.'

'But here I am.' My skull had shattered. Bone fragments pierced my brain. Apparently it was a fine old mess in there. 'Good as new, see?'

'They also told us about Bruce.'

'They told you what?' I ask. 'They know where he is?'

The policewoman presses the heels of her hands against her temples. You'd think I was screaming at her. 'I can't do this,' she says.

'If they know where he is, you have to tell me. Take me to him. Please,' I say. Why the hell do they want to keep it a secret? What's going on? Maybe I should scream after all.

'You really don't know,' the male officer says before I have a chance to fill my lungs. It's clear from the way he rubs his hands together, as if he's washing them, that he's not asking a question. 'We were considering charging you with wasting police time.' He pauses, his hands still, and I try to digest what he's just said. It makes no sense.

'Wasting your time? My son's gone missing. You're supposed to help me find him. Isn't that what you do?'

'Mrs Wilson,' he says. 'Your son was in the car the night you were hit by the drunk driver.'

'I know,' I tell him. 'I know. I know. Me and John and Bruce. We were all in the car.'

'Your son died that night.'

Oh, listen to him, will you? 'Ask for help and this is what I get?' Sweet Jesus. Sweet fucking Jesus.

'Bruce died that night,' the female officer adds, as if saying it enough times will make it true.

The driver's face is all I can see. It's a white blur. I close my eyes just before the cars smash into one another. I wake up in hospital two days later with a terrifying headache.

That's what I remember.

I wipe my eyes.

'I think you should go,' I say.

'Is there anyone we can call?'

'I really think you should go. Now.'

'Mrs Lennox said you were seeing someone. A psychiatrist.'

'Get out. Get the fuck out.'

'We're just trying to help.'

'Get the fuck out!' The female officer approaches me and stretches out a hand, but I bat it away. I know what they're trying to tell me. They're not the first. And they won't be the last.

But they're wrong. My baby's alive and well. I make him a packed lunch every day. I take him to school. I pick him up from school. I take him to the park. I play with him. I have dinner with him. We talk about his daddy. I bathe him. I put him to bed. I read him stories. I do bloody good, all right?

They look at one another and turn to go. 'Clare,' the female officer says. 'You need help.' Her colleague grabs her arm, tugs her towards the door.

'No, I don't,' I whisper. 'I'll find Bruce on my own. I'll find him.'

THE BEST SMALL COUNTRY
IN THE WORLD

Louise Welsh

Henryk couldn't understand what the old man was trying to say to him.

'Are you all right, son?'

The man's lips were pulled back into what might have been a grin, but his harsh tone matched the flint greyness of the world beneath the railway bridge.

'It's just that you look a wee bit out of sorts, if you don't mind me saying so.'

Henryk wanted to walk away. He hadn't eaten since the night before and he was cold. Of course it was colder at home, but the Glasgow chill had a damp quality that had seeped through his trainers, stiffened his feet and crept into his bones.

He couldn't go. If he left the spot now he might miss Tomasz, and there was still an outside chance that it had all been a misunderstanding and Jerzy might yet come back.

'You've been standing here for three hours now. It was the wife that spotted you and sent me down.'

Maybe the old man was asking for money. A dishevelled youth had approached Henryk an hour or so ago nursing a meagre hoard of coppers in a battered polystyrene cup. Henryk had scowled and the thin boy had shambled on. But now that he looked more closely this old man was too well dressed to be a beggar. Cleaner too, his white hair cut short under his tweed cap, a checked scarf tucked neatly into the neck of his padded jacket.

'You want to watch yoursel' round here, son. There's some would have the hide off you if you stop still for too long.'

Henryk moved the old man's hand from his arm and said the few words of English that he knew.

'No . . . no, thank you.'

Tomasz had been angry, more than angry – furious – but Henryk knew in his heart that he'd be back. All he had to do was wait and eventually he would see his friend striding his way through the pedestrians, still angry – Tomasz was often angry and this time the Virgin herself knew he had a right to be – but resigned to facing trouble together.

'You've no' got a clue what I'm rabbiting on about, do you? DO . . . YOU . . . SPEAK . . . ENGLISH?'

Henryk shook his head and moved down the wall a little, but his persecutor's attention had already shifted to an elderly lady in a red coat who was caught midway between the moving traffic. A black cab, like the ones Henryk had seen in movies, stopped to let her cross and she gave a cheery wave to the driver who shook his head resignedly then rolled on.

'Just you wait here a wee minute. That's the wife coming. Now she's seen you're not a suicide bomber she's keen to get her neb in.'

Jerzy's face had invited trust. It was the kind of face used to advertise fresh mint chewing gum of the sort that didn't interfere with your teeth, but whose sugar-freeness didn't mean it wasn't sweet. Henryk had warmed to Jerzy as soon as he had caught sight of him holding up the paper neatly printed with their names at the arrivals gate of Prestwick Airport.

'Look, Tomasz,' he'd said. 'Our chauffeur awaits.'

But Tomasz had merely grunted and given Jerzy the sideways stare he reserved for strangers. It was this look, a look which seemed to hold all their recent difficulties in its reproach, that had sent Henryk's hand into his pocket for the envelope they had both agreed to hold onto until the last possible moment. He had handed it to Jerzy without a single question and so six months of scrimping and self-denial had slipped effortlessly into a stranger's pocket. And with it went some of the glint in the toothpaste-slick smile.

'Okay,' Jerzy had said. 'Come with me.'

And they'd had no choice but to follow.

'I don't think he speaks any English, Jeanette.'

'Is that right?' The old lady looked at Henryk's bag. The tag that had been attached at the airport in Wroclaw was still there. 'Are you lost, son? Look, Tam, he's just off some flight. Are you waiting on a pal?'

'Ach, maybe we shouldn't be bothering him.'

'Of course we should be bothering him. Look at him, he's almost greeting. How would you like it if it was Robert or Kirsty lost somewhere they didn't speak the lingo? I am Scottish.' The old lady pointed at herself. 'Where are you from?' She repeated the action. 'Me Jeanette, me Scottish. You?'

And suddenly he understood what she wanted.

'Henryk. Polski.'

'Henryk Polski.' She gave him a smile, then turned back to her husband. 'He's from Poland.'

'How d'you know?'

'You heard him. *Polski.*'

'That might be his second name. Plenty folk are called after places. Clare English, Joan Sutherland, Ian Paisley.'

'Aye, and Miss Scotland. No, he's Polish right enough. He has a look of that boy that works in Raj's. You know the one? Cheery wee fella.'

'Aye, mibbe, except this one's not looking very cheery.'

'No, he is not.'

Henryk had tried to keep his spirits up as Jerzy had driven them along stretches of motorway that had slowed almost to a standstill as they neared the city.

'It's always this way,' Jerzy had said. 'The first twenty miles fast, the last two slow.'

'The same at home.' Henryk had glanced at Tomasz, hoping he would join the conversation, but his friend's eyes were closed, his head resting against the van window.

Of course it was harder for Tomasz. Henryk was leaving behind his home, his friends and his language, but he was unmarried, his mother still in good health. For him the trip held promises of adventure, the freedom to be himself. Tomasz was leaving behind a good job and years of training. Whatever the tensions at home, the move was always going to hit him harder.

The van drove up a slip road and suddenly the old city was all around them. Tomasz looked up. 'Where are the hills and the heather?'

Jerzy laughed. 'Not so far away. Maybe we'll go to them at the weekend.'

Henryk had noticed Jerzy's expression then and wondered what life here was really like. He had got an impression of cafés and restaurants, a blood red tattoo parlour, the shining glass-front of a theatre. Everything was different from home and, yet, he comforted himself, the substance was the same.

'Okay.' Their driver pulled into a parking space. 'Flat first. You can get washed, have a shave, something to eat and then we'll go to the supermarket where you'll be working.'

They'd unloaded their luggage and Jerzy had led the way. Henryk's bag was heavy, and he was glad when Jerzy finally stopped outside one of the sandstone tenements that lined the street.

'Okay, here we are.'

Tomasz had glanced at the rows of names next to the entry buzzers.

'A lot of people live here.'

Jerzy was fumbling in his jacket pocket.

'It's a workers' district.'

'But no Poles?'

'Two Poles from today.' He took out a set of keys and swore softly. 'Unbelievable. I took the wrong keys from the van. This is for a flat I'm taking people to this afternoon.

I'll have to go back and collect yours. Wait here, I won't be long.'

He gave them the clean, even grin, and then jogged off in the direction of the van. It had been as quick and as casual as that.

Henryk wasn't sure how long they'd stood there before the truth dawned, but he guessed that Tomasz had also clutched the knowledge of their betrayal wordlessly in his chest, still hoping that Jerzy would return, keys in hand, his smile shining.

'Hello, Jeanette, Tam.' An elderly woman laden with shopping bags greeted the couple.

'Oh, no, here we go.' The old man looked at Henryk. 'You'll soon be wishing we'd left you to your misery.'

'Is this your grandson? He's a fine-looking fella, isn't he?'

'Hello, Bella.' The first woman looked important. 'No, this isn't my grandson. Mind you met Robert? They're the same height right enough, but Henryk doesn't look anything like him, Robert's much darker.'

'Oh, aye. So who's this then?'

'We don't know. He's been standing here for almost three hours now. I noticed him when I went out to the shop. That was at eleven, and he was still here when I came back. Then we had a bite to eat and watched a bit of telly. When I went to do the washing up I could see him from the kitchen window. I said to Tam there's something not quite right there and he came down to check on him.'

'And what does he say?'

'Nothing, not a peep, but you can see the way he is.'

The newcomer stared intently into Henryk's face.

'He's awfy glum-looking.' She reached into one of her bags, brought out a packet of biscuits, opened them and thrust them at Henryk. 'Here, a Jaffa Cake can be very sustaining in a crisis.'

'Oh, for goodness' sake.' The old man took a mobile phone out of his pocket and started to dial. 'I should have done this at the off.'

Eventually Tomasz had pressed the door's buzzers. His English was good and though he found the Scottish accents crackling down the entryphone hard to understand, it was clear no one was expecting them, and no one was about to welcome them in with an offer of a bed for the night.

The worst had happened. After all the exchanges of emails and promises, there were no jobs, no lodgings waiting for them in Glasgow. Jerzy had gone, taking their cash and their hopes with him, leaving the two men stranded.

Tomasz had given Henryk a look that was close to a curse.

'Why did I listen to you?'

He turned his back and walked quickly away.

Henryk followed. Men smoking outside pubs tailed them with their eyes and the stream of shoppers parted, giving the couple a wide berth.

'I'm sorry. I shouldn't have given him our money.'

'Supermarket jobs and minimum wage! All just lies. I'm a teacher. What did you expect me to do here? Stack shelves? Collect trolleys?'

They had reached the railway bridge now. Henryk grabbed his friend by the shoulder. Some youths in football strips *ooohed* at them as they passed.

'Kiss and make up!' one of them shouted and his friends laughed.

Henryk ignored the taunts.

'They weren't going to let you teach any more.'

Tomasz pushed him away.

'And whose fault was that?'

He turned and ran, leaving Henryk standing beneath the bridge.

The old people were talking amongst themselves. The woman with the biscuits said, 'Are you sure he's no' up to something? He could be casing a joint.'

Her friend laughed. 'Away with you, he's just a wee, lost boy.'

'A wee, lost Polish boy come to take our jobs.' The woman popped a biscuit into her mouth. 'My Davie says there's too many of them. Sounds like Gdansk round here some days.'

'Your Davie says more than his prayers. They're hard workers, the Poles. My mother said the Polish airmen were always the smartest dressed during the War. All the lassies wanted to dance with them. Them or the Yanks.'

Old Tam harrumphed.

'Aye, your father came back from North Africa to find your house bombed out and your ma with a whole new set of dance moves. Mind, they had a terrible time of it during the War, the Poles . . .'

Their voices drifted into the grumble of passing traffic. Henryk forgot them. Tomasz was coming towards him, flanked by two policemen.

The old man looked up. 'That was quick. I only called youse a minute ago. We're a wee bit concerned about this lad here.'

One of the policemen took out his notebook and asked Tomasz, 'Is this the man who robbed you?'

'No.' Tomasz managed a smile. 'We came here together. We are together.' He squeezed Henryk's shoulder and said in their own language, 'I'm sorry.'

Henryk clasped Tomasz in a brief hug. However hard things were, they would be all right now.

The policeman looked from one to the other, his eyes wary. He nodded, then turned away and said to his partner in a low voice, 'Just a couple of poofs having a domestic.'

Henryk saw Tomasz flinch. He wondered what the policeman had said and how long it would take him, Henryk, to learn English properly. How long before he understood everything.

ONE GOOD TURN

Lin Anderson

The night bus emerged from Princes Street and turned into Lothian Road. Ben watched it pull up at the previous stop and wished once again he'd walked in that direction. At this time of night the buses filled up quickly. He was first in the queue but that might not be enough.

He stole a glance at the people behind him in the bus shelter. A girl, then two guys. The girl looked frozen, her outfit more suited to a nightclub than a February night in Edinburgh. Pretty in a cold, pinched sort of way, she was huddled against the glass as far from the two men as possible, as though she didn't want them to notice her. Difficult in an outfit and heels like that. Ben had already heard their not-so-discreet comments.

The bus was lumbering up the hill, giving Ben the sinking feeling that it was bursting at the seams. He checked his pocket for change, wishing he'd kept enough for a taxi. He could have been home by now, curled up in his warm bed, with the promise of a long lie tomorrow.

The bus slowed as it approached the stop and Ben allowed his hopes to rise. It wouldn't stop if it was full. He stepped out of the shelter and stuck out his hand. Already the others were shuffling forward, eager to get on board. The bus ground to a halt and the door unfolded, blasting them with welcome heat.

'Sorry, one only.'

A chorus of anger erupted behind Ben as the message sank in.

'Fuck you,' the taller of the two guys shouted.

As Ben made to get on, he caught a glimpse of the lassie's frozen face. He thought of his wee sister Catriona wearing shoes she couldn't walk in, ignoring his mum's advice about putting on a coat. He might be frozen but at least he could walk.

'You go.' He stood back to let the girl past.

She hesitated, uncertain how to react. 'You sure?'

'I'll get the next one.'

The door closed behind her taking the heat with it. Ben saw the girl grip the pole, stumbling as the bus pulled sharply away.

'Fucking Good Samaritan,' he cursed himself as he watched the tail end of the bus creep up Lothian Road.

The other two guys had given up and started walking. Ben decided to do the same. God knows when the next bus would arrive, and it too would likely be full. He stuck his hands in his pockets and dipped his head into the biting wind.

Stephanie was so intent on finding something to hold onto that she failed to smile her thanks as the bus pulled away. She felt sorry for the guy who'd given her his place, but was grateful for it.

As the bus accelerated, she widened her stance in an effort to balance on the ridiculous heels, inwardly cursing herself for wearing the stupid shoes. They'd been a mistake; the outfit had been a mistake; the entire night had been a mistake. Dark despair swept over her. Now that she didn't have to concentrate on the cold, the horror that had been her evening came crashing back. She should have listened to her friends. She shouldn't have gone with Gary. Stephanie clutched the pole tighter, her knuckles white.

The bus had pulled up at the traffic lights on the corner of Bread Street. From the right hand window she spotted her Good Samaritan, walking with long swift strides. The sight made her feel a little better. He glanced in, catching her eye and smiling. The bus took off again, moving towards the right-hand lane, heading for Bruntsfield. The guy, already across Bread Street, suddenly broke into a run. Stephanie wanted to cheer him on as he chased the bus to the next traffic light. If it was red, he would catch them up.

Stephanie manoeuvred herself into a position where she could watch his progress from the back window.

The bus wasn't that far ahead. If it met another red at Melville Drive he would easily catch up. The run had warmed him. He was out of breath but not by much, and this was much better than standing at the bus stop. As if in answer to his prayer, the bus slowed. The light was changing. Ben put on an extra spurt.

The two guys appeared from nowhere, slamming hard into him. Ben staggered, his interrupted momentum resounding through his chest.

'Bastard!'

Ben registered the shout and the fact that the two men from the bus stop were circling him. He drew himself up, gasping for breath. 'Sorry,' he said, not sure why he should apologise.

'Aye, you fucking will be!'

Ben felt the sharp point of an elbow bury itself in his ribs. The little air that was left in his lungs escaped with a hiss. A sudden and acute sense of danger told him to get the hell out of there. Never argue. Always run. Before he could obey his own instructions, the two guys were away, whooping and hollering, darting across the road and down the lane towards Fountainbridge.

Ben attempted to straighten up. The bus was still at the lights. If he could get his breath back he could catch it. Somehow that seemed even more important now than before. He drew air painfully into his lungs and set off again. Shit! The bus was beginning to move off. He spotted the girl watching him from the rear window and upped his effort.

He was only yards from the bus when his legs gave way beneath him. He staggered, reaching out to break his fall as the pavement rose abruptly to meet him.

Something had happened. He was on his own then there were three of them. Had he caught up with the other two guys from the bus stop?

Stephanie tried to peer out of the steamed-up windows. He was on his own again, only yards behind the bus, but something was wrong.

'Stop!' she yelled and held her finger on the bell.

*

Ben wondered where he was, and why he was lying down. He remembered. He always felt like this after giving blood. Calm and contented, as though seven pints were all he really needed to survive.

He licked his lips, tasting metal. Salty liquid bubbled up his throat and into his mouth to dribble down his chin. He felt no pain, just a strange burning sensation in his side where the guy had elbowed him. He knew he should get up but had no idea where he would find the strength. He heard the rapid click of heels on the pavement and watched as the shoes ran towards him. Ben found himself wondering again how she could walk on those heels, let alone run.

She dropped onto bare knees beside him. 'Are you all right?'

The face that stared down was frightened and Ben felt the need to reassure her, but couldn't find his voice. Now she was speaking rapidly into her mobile saying something about a stabbing and an ambulance.

Confusion and fear began to devour Ben's sense of calm.

'It's okay.' She reached for his hand and took it in her own. Ben was surprised how warm she felt against his cold skin. He looked up at her. Her eyes were midnight blue. He thought she looked great in spite of the layers of make-up and the daft shoes and wanted to tell her.

'You're going to be all right,' she said, her voice soft and trembling.

It was good to hear her say it, even though Ben knew in that moment it wasn't true.

★

She moved his head onto her knee. Somewhere in the distance, she heard the searing sound of a siren. He had been staring at her, his lips moving, but no sound coming out. She wiped away the red bubble that had formed at the corner of his mouth.

'It's okay, they're coming. Can you hear them?'

Her knees felt warm and she realised it was because she was kneeling in his blood.

She wanted to cry. She wanted to turn the clock back. She wanted to be standing in the freezing wind, watching as the bus pulled away with him inside.

WITH TENDER VIOLENCE
Stuart MacBride

The policeman hates me. I can see it in his eyes. 'Do you understand why you've been arrested?'

I look out the window of the patrol car. The streetlights give the house a washed-out, ill look, like it's dying. Sophie stands on the top step, blood making a thick, dark stain down one side of her face. She cut her head – there's a white gauze pad taped over the gash. Her eyes are red. She's been crying. A petite blonde with big blue eyes and a swollen lip.

I did that.

'I said, do . . . you . . . understand?'

I blink. 'What? I mean, I . . . yes, I understand.'

The policeman nods, then gives my handcuffs one more tug. They're too tight. I complained when they put them on, but it didn't make any difference.

He scowls. 'People like you make me sick.'

I almost say something, but he's right. This is what I deserve.

Sophie holds out her hand and Monica runs to her. Four years old, dressed in her fluffy blue pyjamas, clutching Mr Bunnyfish. My daughter looks at the police car with wide eyes. Watching as the man in the black uniform and stabproof vest slams the back door, then climbs in behind the wheel.

His partner is on the radio, telling the station that I'm being brought in; that I'll need to see the duty doctor.

Then the car pulls away from the kerb and Sophie stares right at me. I can almost hear her thoughts from here:

Never again. It's going to be different from now on. You dirty, fucking bastard.

I look away. She's right. She's always right.

It's June and we're walking down Balmedie beach, hand in hand. Sophie looks radiant, her yellow cotton dress fluttering in the breeze, like she's wearing sunshine. Andrew's playing a game of dare with the North Sea, running after the retreating water, then scampering back when the next wave comes in. He's five, and when he grows up, he wants to be a lion.

Yeah, good luck with that.

Sophie stops, and the sand is warm around my bare feet as she reaches up and pulls me down for a kiss.

Jesus, she's just . . . stunning.

I tell her I love her. And I mean it.

I really do.

It's February and my palm slams into her cheek. Her head snaps round and blood flies from her bottom lip. Her hand goes to her mouth and she stares at me, with shocked eyes.

It's three hours later and I'm sitting in a grubby room, waiting for the duty doctor to finish talking to a detective inspector who hates me almost as much as the policeman in the corner does.

Stinks in here.

Someone's tried covering up the smell with air-freshener,

but it just lies on top of the stench: BO, cigarettes and the cloying reek of artificial flowers. Can barely breathe . . .

There's a camera bolted to the wall, watching me with its dead, black eye. Reflecting back the worthless piece of crap I've become.

A man who hits his wife is not a real man.

The doctor stops talking and the inspector peers round the door at me.

I try to move my seat, but it's bolted to the floor.

None of this would have happened if I didn't love her so much.

It's July and it's raining. It should always rain at funerals. I stand in the downpour and watch as they lower Andrew into the ground.

Didn't even get to see his sixth birthday. Never got to become a lion.

Sophie's not here. The doctors think it'd be too much of a strain in her condition. So instead it's just me and the family I haven't seen for four years. None of them really knowing what to say. Everyone's in tears, my mum, stepdad, brothers . . . The minister's eyes are red. He wipes them with the sleeve of his cassock when he thinks no one's looking.

So why can't I cry?

They're burying my son and I can't even cry.

What the hell is wrong with me?

*

'So, Frank,' says the woman on the other side of the interview room table, 'this isn't the first time you've been in trouble with the law, is it?'

Her breath smells of cigarettes and coffee. She doesn't look like a detective inspector, she looks like a tramp in a shiny grey suit, her hair all rumpled and random.

I shrug. 'Couple of parking tickets.'

'Oh no, no, no . . .' She smiles at me with yellowy teeth. 'I'm talking about something a wee bittie more serious than leaving the family Volvo on a double yellow. I'm talking about Andrew. Remember him?'

It's July and Andrew isn't moving. He's lying at the bottom of the stairs, one leg draped over the bottom step. His head's twisted around so he's looking straight back over his shoulder. Eyes open.

'Andrew?'

He's not moving.

'Come on Andrew, this isn't fucking funny!'

I reach out and touch his pale skin. It's cold.

There's a horrible sound: painful . . . tearing. Like someone's soul is being sandblasted. It takes me a long time to realise it's coming from me. I'm on my knees in the hall screaming.

The detective inspector checks the manila file on the interview room table. 'Broken neck. Broken leg. Broken arm.

Three cracked ribs.' She pulls a photo out and slaps it in front of me.

Andrew, lying on his back on a stainless steel surface. His eyes deader than the camera bolted to the wall.

'You know what I think?' says the DI. 'I think we should take another good, long look at how Andrew ended up like that. After all: man beats the living hell out of his wife, who knows what he's capable of?'

I can't look at her. 'I didn't hurt Andrew.'

'Your wife's what, five-one, five-two? Can't weigh more than eight stone. You proud of what you did?'

I've not been proud of anything for a long, long time.

Sophie's head smashes into the mirror. Shards fall in slow motion, each one reflecting a bitter slice of pain and misery.

I try to move, but my legs don't work any more.

The doorbell rings again.

Mirrored glass hits the carpet and she staggers backwards. Falls. Crashes against the sideboard, sending ornaments flying.

The ceramic cat I bought her for our last anniversary shatters.

Sophie screams.

Blood streams down her face.

Someone hammers on the front door. 'Police! Open up! Open up *now*!'

★

The inspector's right. What happened to Andrew was my fault. I know because Sophie told me so.

The inspector comes back into the interview room, shutting the door behind her. The duty doctor stays outside. Coward.

She clears her throat and leans on the back of her chair. 'Take off your shirt.'

'I . . . no.'

He's told her.

How could he tell her? What happened to doctor–patient confidentiality?

She sighs, then tells the policeman who hates me to suspend the interview and switch off the tapes. 'Take off your shirt, Frank.'

'I can't.'

'Take your bloody shirt off!'

Sophie's face is red and blotchy. She stands in the kitchen waving a pair of lacy black knickers in my face, screaming, 'Who is she? How could you do this to me? To us – your family?'

I've never seen them before. I tell her. I swear to God. I get on my knees and beg her to believe me.

'What's Andrew going to think when he finds out his father's fucking some whore?'

My fingers fumble with the buttons. It's not easy with the handcuffs on, but eventually I manage. Then sit there, shirt hanging open, the fabric brushing the sides of my chest.

The inspector takes a breath, then says, 'Jesus . . .'

Sophie lurches into the living room, a smile stretching her face wide. She's been drinking, I can smell it from here. 'Frankie! Frankie, have I told you lately that I love you?'

She's drunk. And happy. For now. But that can change faster than you could believe. 'I do, I love you *sooooo* much.'

She drops her keys on the sideboard, then checks her blotchy face in the mirror. 'Do you . . . Do you love me, Frankie?'

'Yes.' I smile, hoping that her good mood will hold. 'Of course I love you.'

She runs a finger across her eyebrow. Then turns. 'Then why are you such a FUCKING SHIT?'

Oh God . . .

The detective inspector stares at my chest. I know what she's thinking: he's disgusting, how could any woman ever want *that*? All those scars, the cigarette burns, the rough patch of skin where a pan of boiling pasta caught me in the ribs. Scalded and ugly. As disfigured on the outside as I am on the inside.

'Holy shit.'

I close my eyes.

'Who the hell did this to you?'

'No one. It was an accident.'

She's screaming, kicking, swearing. I back away, covering my face and head with my arms. Making sure the bruises land where I can cover them up. Keep them hidden.

'You're fucking useless! You hear me, Frank? Useless! You've *always* been useless!'

'Please, don't . . .'

'Why do you think I have to screw other men, Frank? Because you can't get the job done, can you? Because you're so *fucking* pathetic!'

Something heavy smashes down on my elbow and I cry out.

'Weak and useless!'

This time it catches me on the side of the head. Yellow. Noise, a booming noise.

'Why have I put up with you all this time? Well?'

'I'm . . . sorry.' The world is going in and out on a riptide of white noise and nausea. 'I didn't mean to . . .'

'You don't really think you managed to get me pregnant, do you? 'Cause you didn't. It was James. He's Monica's *real* dad, because you're just . . . fucking . . . pathetic! I wouldn't let your filthy seed sprout inside me again. Not after that little shit Andrew.'

I try to get away, to stagger into the hall, but she hits me with the iron griddle pan again.

'He was a dirty little bastard, just . . . like . . . you.'

My back thumps into the wall and I stop. Nowhere left to run.

She steps forward slowly, her voice lowered to a throaty whisper. 'He deserved what he got.'

And I snap. Just like that. I take my hand and I slap that vicious look off her face. Her head snaps round and blood flies from her bottom lip. Her hand goes to her mouth and she stares at me, with shocked eyes.

'You hit me? YOU FUCKING HIT ME!'

Sophie grabs the phone out of its cradle.

'I'm sorry, I'm so sorry, I didn't mean to . . .'

'Hello, police? I need the police. My husband's trying to kill me!'

'It was a mistake, Sophie, I . . .'

She gives them the address, looking at me the whole time, then hangs up. 'The police are on their way, Frank. They'll take you away and lock you up where you can't hurt your family any more. You'll never see Monica again. Bastards like you get raped in the showers. But you'll like that, won't you? Dirty little fuck.'

She keeps it up until the police ring the doorbell. I know it's them because I can see the blue and white lights flashing through the Venetian blinds.

'They'll lock you up and throw away the key . . .'

'Sophie, please, it was a mistake. I didn't mean to hit you!'

She draws herself up to her full five foot two and a quarter, smiles at me, then head-butts the mirror.

Shards fall in slow motion, each one reflecting a bitter

slice of pain and misery. Her face is covered in blood, and she's giggling. 'Who do you think the police are going to believe now?'

She stands at the top of the stairs, looking down at Andrew. He's not moving. Why isn't he moving? Oh Jesus . . .

'See what you made me do?'

I'm in the kitchen, staring into the bin. An Ann Summers plastic bag lies half-buried under a mound of potato peelings. I reach in and pull the bag out, open it, and find a receipt for one pair of lacy black knickers.

'Well, it's your lucky day,' says the detective inspector, settling back against the wall of my cell. 'Your wife's not pressing charges. Apparently it was all a big mistake. She slipped and fell against the mirror.'

I don't say anything.

It smells of vomit in here. That was my fault, too.

'That what happened to you, Frank? You slip and fall all those times? That where you get all them scars from?'

'Can I go now?'

The detective inspector closes her eyes, and pinches the bridge of her nose. 'Doesn't have to be like this, Frank.'

'I . . . I just want to go home.'

Sophie is waiting for me at the front door to the station. A small dot of red has oozed through the gauze pad on her forehead. She hugs me, kisses me, promises me it'll never happen again.

'It's going to be different from now on,' she says.

Just like she always does.

THE ROAD TAKEN

Gillian Galbraith

I am ashamed to admit that it arrived at the very moment that he did, this constant need, this compulsion, to observe him. With all my heart I wish that I could say otherwise, I wish that I could say that my first reaction on seeing him was one of pure, unadulterated, maternal love. Because that is how it should have been, how my mother had described it and how I had hoped and prayed that it would be. But the truth is very different, and it has shaped both our lives. Although he was born over eighteen years ago, eighteen years, three months, five days and four hours ago to be exact, I still remember everything about that day with complete clarity.

At 10 a.m. on 4 June 1990 I lay, frightened and immobile, on the operating table, an unexplained space where any partner might be, as the radio in the theatre blasted out some cover version of 'That'll Be the Day'. An Irish nurse, smelling strongly of fried onions, busied herself erecting a horizontal screen across my shoulders to ensure that I could see no further than six inches from my chin. Having finished her task, she took my hand in hers, then moved a strand of my hair out of my eyes. Meanwhile unseen fingers appeared to be rummaging around inside my abdomen as if searching in an old handbag for a lost purse. After about five minutes of rummaging, the surgeon raised my clay-coloured child triumphantly above his head, as if it were some kind of football trophy, and as I looked at the baby, in all his nakedness, I felt my heart slowly sink. Glistening like a little seal, he was placed on my breast and, thinking that he had found a safe refuge, he closed his milky eyes once more and emitted a small, contented mew. But my eyes remained open, wide open, as I stroked the curve of his tiny spine, all the while scrutinising the creature whose skin was now warming my own.

He had black, spiky hair, a sallow complexion and a disproportionately large nose. I do not know who, if anyone, he then looked like but one thing was quite obvious and that was that he did not look like me or mine. As I studied him so dispassionately, it did not worry me that I felt no love towards him – after all I did not yet know him – and a few of the other mothers on the ward appeared equally detached, equally bemused, by the new life they had created. In between waves of sleep, I glanced down at him, deliberately inhaling the air around him, growing accustomed to his scent and murmuring his name. Adam.

On waking he 'latched on', as the midwives insisted on describing it, to my right nipple and exerted every ounce of his newborn strength in his search for milk. When, finally, he fell asleep once more, his belly now rounded and tight as a balloon, I eased his slack lips off and examined the bruises and grazes that he had inflicted on me. The sight of them gave me a strange kind of comfort. A proper mother, the sort that I aspired to be, would think nothing of such injury, such pain, instead rejoicing in her ability to sustain her infant. I believed I had passed that first test with flying colours.

Months and years passed and I never took his existence for granted, always felt the need to watch him, and that impulse grew stronger, as he did. Sometimes, when we were in public places, a park or a shopping centre, I would catch another woman's eye and she would smile at me like a co-conspirator. What she saw was a mother doing her job, watching over a precious child, unable to wrest her eyes from its perfect beauty. But that is not what was happening.

And from the very start, despite my best intentions, I am ashamed to say that my mind was never open about Adam. I knew what he might become. Throughout my son's childhood, others used to tell me what an exceptionally kind individual he was, such a sensitive boy, so thoughtful. But I never believed a word they said. He might fool them but not me.

I could not bring myself to love him. I was far too busy watching him. Once, when he was about six, we looked together into the bathroom mirror, our heads touching, side by side. I rolled my ice-blue eyes round and round in their sockets and he followed suit, his dark irises following mine. Still staring at my reflected face, suddenly conscious of the difference in our looks, he asked about his father and I told him, as I had done before, that we had loved each other very much and that but for the traffic accident we would all be together now. He liked that idea, and so did I.

The people in my pew, on either side of me now, evidently loved Adam. I can see it in their faces, furtive tears escaping from their eyes, brows furrowed in sorrow. Occasionally, a muffled sob reaches my ears from the row behind me, too. In amongst the known, his schoolfriends and their parents, are others, a few that I recognise but cannot place, and there are many unknown to me, too. The kirk is full, and those that could find no place inside wait outside in the pouring rain, joining in the hymns a few bars behind the rest of the congregation. His name is on the order of service, above the dates of his birth and death, and I have called it 'A Service of Thanksgiving'.

I know that if I had been stronger, better, everything could have been different but I do not chastise myself for my weakness too often – it changes nothing. The minister told me that sometimes weights are placed upon us that we cannot bear. Those around me singing 'Love Divine All Loves Excelling' so lustily, remain mystified by his death. A young man in his prime like that. But there is no mystery to it. The first policeman that I came across inside our house, still shaken, pale from cutting the body down, asked me gently if Adam had left a note. I shook my head. Of course, there was no note; he did not need to leave one. We both knew why.

All I can say in my own defence, and I count it as nothing, was that I was tired, exhausted, after a long day at work. He ambled into the kitchen, a broad grin on his face, holding out his pay packet to me, the fruits of his second week in yet another job-trial. Still beaming, and with beer on his breath, he told me that Mr Gray, the boss, was really pleased with him, thought he had 'great potential' and might 'go far'. Without thought I allowed a dismissive, sceptical sound to escape my lips. I had heard it all before. In response he instinctively pushed me, just the lightest touch really, because he was angered . . . no, hurt, by my reaction. And then he began berating me, shouting, swearing, railing against the lack of a father, screaming that his life would have been so much better with a dad, and, then, assuring me, as he had done on countless earlier occasions, that his father would have understood him, would have been proud of him.

Until the day I die, I will remember the cold, sarcastic tone I adopted when I replied to him and that, along with what I said, can never be forgiven. 'Your father would have understood you . . .' I began slowly, deliberately, '. . . and would, certainly, be proud of you. Maybe not so much for doing well in your job but certainly for pushing me. He was violent towards women, too. That's all I know about him. I only met him once . . . in Cockburn Street, in the dark and in the rain. I was seventeen, returning home after a party and he . . . well, he was on the lookout . . .'

Hearing myself I nearly stopped, but, catching sight of his angry features, I carried on. It was as if in the middle of drowning, he had somehow managed to raise his head above the water for air and I had a choice – push his head back under the waves or cradle it in my arms and let him breathe. But I was tired and angry, sick of carrying around the weight of a huge lie.

'. . . and he found me, raped me and left me bleeding on the cobbles. And that single meeting with that man, your father, resulted in you. And they never caught him either . . . Apparently, my description was not good enough.'

Adam's dark eyes watched me, frantically examining my face. Their expression was easy to read. Let it not be true, let it not be true. And in that moment I was given a second chance, and if I had been stronger, better, I would have, somehow, found a way to retract, to soften that vicious truth, but I failed and pushed his head below the water again. In fact, I felt oddly triumphant, vindicated. From the moment of his birth I had believed that he would turn out like his father and here, at last, was the proof that had always been missing. After all, this 'gentle', 'sensitive' boy had just assaulted me, his own mother.

One of the undertakers is signalling for me to leave my pew and I stumble on my way out as if blinded by tears, and I know what the row upon row of mourners see. They see, simply, the grief-stricken mother and, of course, I am. But, I am much, much more than that. I am also my son's killer.

Last night I stayed awake trying to excuse myself, forgive myself, reminding myself that when I made the decision to keep my son I was only seventeen, knew nothing, under-stood nothing. I was too young, too naive, to anticipate the years of lies, evasions and embarrassments that lay ahead. Never mind understand my own limitations.

And at precisely what age do you tell your child that his father raped you? He never seemed quite old enough to discover such a legacy, never mind cope with it. Once, when he was fifteen, I began to edge towards the subject, but seeing his trusting eyes looking into mine, I could not bring myself to deliver such a blow and stepped back again, convincing myself that he did not need this information yet. At sixteen he seemed equally fragile, at seventeen the same. He used to speculate on the characteristics he must have inherited from his dad: his neatness, his ease with people, his ability with maps. They were all good. How would he view himself when he found out the truth?

Throughout the years I had with Adam I sometimes used to wonder how my life might have been if it had never happened; if I had not decided to take a short cut down Cockburn Street or had left the party twenty minutes later, or twenty minutes earlier. The most likely scenario, I decided, was that I would have gone to university as I had planned, graduated, then found work in a lab maybe, met a fellow scientist or technician, married him and had two or three children. If I indulge my fantasy further, I see the day when my children have children, and I and my balding husband become doting grandparents. The dream is not too extravagant, I think, not so far removed from the ordinary lives of others. It should not have been too much to ask. But my reality was different, less rosy, more barren. I never married nor had any kind of intimate relationship with a man because I was too afraid. Since my parents died, thirteen years ago, it's been just the two of us, Adam and me. I did not know myself when I was seventeen, I did not know my only son, dared not love him and now, I do not know how I will live without him.

VOICES THROUGH THE WALL
Alex Gray

Voices through the wall. I can hear them, whispering, making insinuations about me. But I'm well used to that now, aren't I? The constant babble of tongues, the sly, invisible eyes looking at the plasterboard that divides them from me, knowing I can sense their disapproval.

It wasn't always like this, though. When he was born, it wasn't thought of as a crime any more; having a wee one out of wedlock had become as common as setting up house together with your man. There was no parental opposition either, because both of mine were long dead. No grannies to shush the wee fella or to take him off my hands for a brief hour while I caught up with washing his baby clothes. Just him and me. Didn't do too badly, either. Got a flat off the council, one floor up, and managed to furnish it with second-hand stuff from the Sally Army shop in Partick. Visiting officer from the Social helped an' all. Nice woman she was, telling me it was my right to have all these things; the layette, the blankets and even the living room decorated at their expense.

So it was nice at first, having this wee man cuddling up, me the centre of his universe. He was never a quiet baby and squirmed and wriggled whenever it was time to change a filthy nappy but he loved splashing in the blue plastic bath, making damp patches on the worn carpet. Never had any bother from them downstairs, either. No-one banging on the ceiling to tell me the racket was too much, making the baby scream even louder. No, the neighbours were lovely; even brought nicely wrapped gifts for Johnny at

Christmas. Made me feel bad 'cause I had nothing to give them back. I remember the yellow rubber duck and that teddy bear with his knitted blue waistcoat: Johnny played with them for years until they were all but trashed. They disappeared one day after he came home from school and I never found them till just the other day, at the bottom of a box in the hall cupboard. Teddy's head was missing and the duck would never bob in the water any more, its plastic sides stabbed through with holes. Holding them in both hands, I wept tears that I had thought could not be shed any more.

Most days I go down to the chapel, but not when Father is in the middle of a service. No, I wait until I'm sure there's nobody left then slip into a pew at the front and have my conversation with the Madonna. Doesn't look as if she could say much, this painted plaster figure, but it does me good to talk to her. She understands, you see. *What was it like for you?* I sometimes ask her. *Did they mock you and whisper behind their hands?* 'That's his mother. Bad lot, if you ask me. No way to bring up a child. Illegitimate, an' all.' *Did they point their fingers at you? Wag their self-righteous heads and tell themselves, 'It all comes down to the parents, in the end.' Aye, I can guess the sort of pain that pierced your heart after they put him on a cross and killed him.*

They didn't kill Johnny, just put him away. The lawyer told me he'd get life. Not that it really means life, you know. Just a couple of decades and he could've been back out. But that was before they'd assessed him and found that he wasn't right in the head. Not his fault he'd murdered those wee girls, really. Something in his brain that was never right. But it doesn't stop the voices, on and on, wondering whether I was a bad mother to him, making him what he is today.

The newspapers had a field day. This woman came up to see me, promising a load of cash if I would tell them my story. I told her to go to hell. It wasn't any of their business, was it? When I had to appear in court as a witness, they wouldn't leave me alone. I saw the wee girls' parents, two mums and two dads, heads bowed as they entered the High Court. Recognised them from the papers and the telly. Their lives would never be the same again. Never. But neither would mine, and the thought that they might just understand made me want to go up to them and say I was sorry, as if apologising for what Johnny had done could make it okay. I never did get close enough to catch the eye of any one of them, though their misery cut me to ribbons.

I'd said sorry so many times before. To the weans who'd been bullied by my son and to the parents who'd come knocking at my door, fierce scowls on their unforgiving faces. *Sorry*, I'd say, trying to smile. *He's just a very active boy*, I'd tell them, thinking to myself, *wild, uncontrollable*, not the wee lad who'd crawled into my bed whenever the thunder crashed and the rain drummed against the windowpanes. When had it all gone wrong?

Primary Five he'd been escorted home by the head

teacher of St Francis. There had been a fight and Johnny had pulled out a blade. *Was it one that I recognised?* the man had asked. Looking at my wee vegetable knife, I'd said, yes, it was. Johnny had hung his head and said nothing at all, nodding his promises to be a better student, never to carry a dangerous weapon like that again. I threw the knife out and bought another one in Woolworth's. Somehow I couldn't bear the thought of cutting up potatoes with the same blade that my son had used to hurt another little boy. But it hadn't stopped there. Money went missing from my purse and into Johnny's pocket. He must have bought his first switchblade with cash from his very own family allowance. And by the time I challenged him about it, he had grown bigger than me and looked down at his wee maw with a sneer on his face that was so different from the lovely boy I'd once known.

They said I should have controlled him better. Been a role model for him, whatever that meant. But he left home at sixteen, no qualifications to his name, ready to face a world on his own. I'd cried then, but there was also a sense of pride that my boy could stand on his own two feet. He got a job, and came back sometimes for a meal or just to tell me how he was doing. Half of me wanted him back home but the other half felt only relief once he'd gone again.

It was Mother's Day today. For the last week I've seen the shops full of decorated banners and cards, flowers in the doorways. Johnny made me a card in Primary Two. I took it out this morning and looked at it, his childish scrawl wishing me a *Happy Mother's Day*. I don't have any letters from the place he's in, not even a Christmas card. And I'm not allowed to send anything in case it upsets him. Sometimes I wonder what it's like for him in that place full of mad, bad, sick people and the doctors who have to restrain their violent behaviour. Does Johnny hear voices through the walls there? And can he hear the whispering coming into his room at night?

The sound of the television stops and the muttering begins, telling me I'm a bad mother, that it's all my fault, that these little girls would be alive if it hadn't been for me. And they will go on, whispering their insinuations even when my dust blows away and this victim is long forgotten.

OUT OF THE FLESH

Christopher Brookmyre

Restorative Justice, they cry it. That's what happens when wee scrotes like you get sat doon wi' their victims, *mano a mano*, kinda like you and me are daein' the noo. It's a matter of talking and understanding, as opposed tae a chance for the likes ay me tae batter your melt in for tryin' tae tan ma hoose. The idea is that us victims can put a face tae the cheeky midden that wheeched wur stereos, and youse can see that the gear you're pochlin' actually belongs tae somebody. Cause you think it's a gemme, eh? Just aboot no' gettin' caught, and anyway the hooses are insured, so it's naebody's loss, right? So the aim is tae make you realise that it's folk you're stealin' frae, and that it does a lot mair damage than the price ay a glazier and a phone call tae Direct Line.

Aye. Restorative justice. Just a wee blether tae make us baith feel better, that's the idea. Except it normally happens efter the courts and the polis are through wi' their end, by 'mutual consent' and under 'official supervision'. Cannae really cry this mutual consent, no' wi' you tied tae that chair. But restorative justice is whit you're gaunny get.

Aye. You're shitin your breeks 'cause you think I'm gaunny leather you afore the polis get here, then make up whatever story I like. Tempting, I'll grant you, but ultimately nae guid. See, the point aboot restorative justice is that it helps the baith ay us. Me batterin your melt in isnae gaunny make you think you're a mug for tannin' hooses, is it? It's just gaunny make ye careful the next time, when ye come back wi' three chinas and a big chib.

Believe me, you're lucky a batterin's aw you're afraid of, ya wee nyaff. Whit I'm gaunny tell you is worth mair than anythin' you were hopin' tae get away wi' frae here, an' if you're smart, you'll realise what a big favour I'm daein' ye.

Are you sittin' uncomfortably? Then I'll begin.

See, I used tae be just like you. Surprised are ye? Nearly as surprised as when you tried tae walk oot ae this living room and found yoursel wi' a rope roon ye. I've been around and about, son. I never came up the Clyde in a banana boat and I wasnae born sixty, either. Just like you, did I say? Naw. Much worse. By your age I'd done mair hooses than the census. This was in the days when they said you could leave your back door open, and tae be fair, you could, as long as you didnae mind me and ma brer Billy nippin' in and helpin' oursels tae whatever was oan offer.

We werenae frae the village originally; we were frae the Soothside. Me and Billy hud tae move in wi' oor uncle when ma faither went inside. Two wee toerags, fifteen and fourteen, frae a tenement close tae rural gentility. It wasnae so much fish oot ay watter as piranhas in a paddlin' pool. Easy pickin's, ma boy, easy pickin's. Open doors, open windaes, open wallets. Course, the problem wi' bein' piranhas in a paddlin' pool is it's kinda obvious whodunnit. At the end of the feedin' frenzy, when the watter's aw red, naebody's pointin' any fingers at the nearest Koi carp, know what I'm sayin'? But you'll know yoursel', when you're that age, it's practically impossible for the polis or the courts tae get a binding result, between the letter ay the law and the fly moves ye can pull. Didnae mean ye were immune fae a good leatherin' aff the boys in blue, right enough, roon the back ay the station, but that's how I know applied retribution's nae use as a disincentive. Efter a good kickin', me and Billy were even mair determined tae get it up them; just meant we'd try harder no tae get caught.

But then wan night, aboot October time, the Sergeant fronts up while me and Billy are kickin' a baw aboot. Sergeant, no less. Royalty. Gold-plated boot in the baws comin' up, we think. But naw, instead he's aw nicey-nicey, handin' oot fags, but keepin' an eye over his shoulder, like he doesnae want seen.

And by God, he doesnae. Fly bastard's playin' an angle, bent as a nine-bob note.

'I know the score, boys,' he says. 'What's bred in the bone, will not out of the flesh. Thievin's in your nature: I cannae change that, your uncle cannae change that, and when yous are auld enough, the jail willnae change that. So we baith might as well accept the situation and make the best ay it.'

'Whit dae ye mean?' I asks.

'I've a wee job for youse. Or mair like a big job, something tae keep ye in sweeties for a wee while so's ye can leave folk's hooses alane. Eejits like you are liable tae spend forever daein' the same penny-ante shite, when there's bigger prizes oan offer if you know where tae look.'

Then he lays it aw oot, bold as brass. There's a big hoose,

a mansion really, a couple ay miles ootside the village. Me and Billy never knew it was there; well, we'd seen the gates, but we hadnae thought aboot what was behind them, 'cause you couldnae see anythin' for aw the trees. The owner's away in London, he says, so the housekeeper and her husband are bidin' in tae keep an eye oan the place. But the Sergeant's got the inside gen that the pair ay them are gaun tae some big Hallowe'en party in the village. Hauf the toon's gaun, in fact, includin' him, which is a handy wee alibi for while we're daein' his bidding.

There was ayeways a lot o' gatherings among the in-crowd in the village, ma uncle tell't us. Shady affairs, he said. Secretive, like. He reckoned they were up tae all sorts, ye know? Wife-swappin' or somethin'. Aw respectable on the ootside, but a different story behind closed doors. Course, he would say that, seein' as the crabbit auld bugger never got invited.

Anyway, the Sergeant basically tells us it's gaunny be carte blanche. This was the days before fancy burglar alarms an' aw that shite, remember, so we'd nothin' tae worry aboot regards security. But he did insist on somethin' a bit strange, which he said was for all of oor protection: we'd tae 'make it look professional, but no' too professional'. We understood what he meant by professional: don't wreck the joint or dae anythin' that makes it obvious whodunnit. But the 'too professional' part was mair tricky, it bein' aboot disguisin' the fact it was a sortay inside job.

'Whit ye oan aboot?' I asked him. 'Whit's too professional? Polishin' his flair and giein' the woodwork a dust afore we leave?'

'I'm talkin' aboot bein' canny whit you steal. The man's got things even an accomplished burglar wouldnae know were worth a rat's fart – things only valuable among collectors, so you couldnae fence them anyway. I don't want you eejits knockin' them by mistake, 'cause it'll point the finger back tae the village. If you take them, he'll know the thief had prior knowledge, as opposed tae just hittin' the place because it's a country mansion.'

'So whit are these things?'

'The man's a magician – oan the stage, like. That's whit he's daein' doon in London. He's in variety in wan o' thae big West End theatres. But that's just show business, how he makes his money. The word is, he's intae some queer, queer stuff, tae dae wi' the occult.'

'Like black magic?'

'Aye. The man's got whit ye cry "artefacts". Noo, I'm no' sayin' ye'd be naturally inclined tae lift them, and I'm no' sure you'll even come across them, 'cause I don't know where they're kept, but I'm just warnin' you tae ignore them if ye dae. Take the cash, take gold, take jewels, just the usual stuff – and leave anythin' else well enough alone.'

'Got ye.'

'And wan last thing, boys: if you get caught, this conversation never took place. Naebody'd believe your word against mine anyway.'

So there we are. The inside nod on a serious score and

a guarantee frae the polis that it's no' gaunny be efficiently investigated. Sounded mair like Christmas than Hallowe'en, but it pays tae stay a wee bit wary, especially wi' the filth involved – and bent filth at that, so we decided tae ca' canny.

Come the big night, we took the wise precaution of takin' a train oot the village, and mair importantly made sure we were *seen* takin' it by the station staff. The two piranhas had tae be witnessed gettin' oot ae the paddlin' pool, for oor ain protection. We bought return tickets tae Glesca Central, but got aff at the first stop, by which time the inspector had got a good, alibi-corroboratin' look at us. We'd planked two stolen bikes behind a hedge aff the main road earlier in the day, and cycled our way back, lyin' oot flat at the side ay the road the odd time a motor passed.

It took longer than we thought, mainly because it was awfy dark and you cannae cycle very fast when you cannae see where you're goin'. We liked the dark, me and Billy. It suited us, felt natural tae us, you know? But that night just seemed thon wee bit blacker than usual, maybe because we were oot in the countryside. It was thon wee bit quieter as well, which made me feel kinda exposed, like I was a wee moose and some big owl was gaunny swoop doon wi' nae warnin' and huckle us away for its tea.

And that was *before* we got tae the hoose.

'Bigger prizes,' we kept sayin' tae each other. 'Easy money.' But it didnae feel like easy anythin' efter we'd climbed ower the gates, believe me. If we thought it was dark on the road, that was nothin' compared tae in among

thae tall trees. Then we saw the hoose. Creepy as, I'm tellin'
you. Looked twice the size it would have in daylight an'
all, towerin' above us like it was leanin' ower tae check us
oot. And on the top floor a light wis oan in wan wee windae.

'There's somebody in, Rab,' Billy says. 'The game's a bogey.
Let's go hame.'

A very tempting notion, I'll admit, but no' as tempting
as playin' pick 'n' mix in a mansion full o' goodies.

'Don't be a numpty,' I says. 'They've just left a light oan
by mistake. As if there wouldnae be lights on doonstairs
if somebody was hame. C'mon.'

'Aye, aw right,' Billy says, and we press on. We make
oor way roon the back, lookin' for a likely wee windae.
Force of habit, gaun roon the back, forgettin' there's
naebody tae see us if we panned in wan o' the ten-footers
at the front. I'm cuttin' aboot lookin' for a good-sized
stane tae brek the glass, when Billy reverts tae the mair
basic technique of just tryin' the back door, which swings
open easy as you like. Efter that, it's through and intae
the kitchen, where we find some candles and matches.
Billy's aw for just stickin' the lights oan as we go, but I'm
still no' sure that sneaky bastard Sergeant isnae gaunny
come breengin' in wi' a dozen polis any minute, so I'm
playin' it smart.

Oot intae the hallway and I'm soon thinkin', knackers
tae smart, let there be light. The walls just disappear
up intae blackness; I mean, there had tae be a ceiling up
there somewhere, but Christ knows how high. Every

footstep's echoin' roon the place, every breath's bein' amplified like I'm walkin' aboot inside ma ain heid. But maistly it was the shadows . . . Aw, man, thae shadows. I think fae that night oan, I'd rather be in the dark than in candle-light, that's whit the shadows were daein' tae me. And aw the time, of course, it's gaun through my mind, the Sergeant's words – 'queer, queer stuff . . . the occult'. Black magic. Doesnae help that it's Hallowe'en, either, every bugger tellin' stories aboot ghosts and witches aw week.

But I tell myself: screw the nut, got a job tae dae here. Get oan wi' it, get oot, and we'll be laughin' aboot this when we're sittin' on that last train hame frae Central. So we get busy, start tannin' rooms. First couple are nae use. I mean, quality gear, but nae use tae embdy withoot a furniture lorry. Then third time lucky: intae this big room wi' aw these display cabinets. A lot ay it's crystal and china – again, nae use, but we can see the Sergeant wisnae haverin'. There's jewellery, ornaments: plenty of gold and silver and nae shortage of gemstones embedded either.

'If it sparkles, bag it,' I'm tellin' Billy, and we're laughin' away until we baith hear somethin'. It's wan o' thae noises ye cannae quite place: cannae work oot exactly whit it sounded like or where it wis comin' frae, but you know you heard it: deep, rumbling, low.

'Whit was that?'

'You heard it an' aw?'

'Aye. Ach, probably just the wind,' I says, no even kiddin' masel.

'Wis it fuck the wind. It sounded like a whole load ay people singin' or somethin'.'

'Well I cannae hear it noo, so never bother.'

'Whit aboot that light? Whit if somebody *is* up there?'

'It didnae sound like it came frae above. Maist likely the plumbing. The pipes in these big auld places can make some weird sounds.'

Billy doesnae look so sure, but he gets on wi' his job aw the same.

We go back tae the big hallway, but stop and look at each other at the foot of the stairs. We baith know what the other's thinkin': there's mair gear tae be had up there, but neither ay us is in a hurry tae go lookin' for it. That said, there's still room in the bags, and I'm about to suggest we grasp the thistle when we hear the rumblin' sound again. Could be the pipes, I'm thinkin', but I know what Billy meant when he said a load ay folk singin'.

'We're no' finished doon here,' I says, postponin' the issue a wee bit, and we go through another door aff the hall. It's a small room, compared tae the others anyway, and the curtains are shut, so I reckon it's safe tae stick the light oan. The light seems dazzling at first, but that's just because we'd become accustomed tae the dark. Cannae be more than forty-watt. There's a big desk in the middle, a fireplace on wan wall and bookshelves aw the way tae the ceiling, apart frae where the windae is.

Billy pulls a book aff the shelf, big ancient-lookin' leather-bound effort. 'Have a swatch at this,' he says, pointin' tae the open page. 'Diddies! Look.'

He's right. There's a picture ay a wummin in the scud lyin' doon oan a table; no' a photie, like, a drawin', an' aw this queer writin' underneath, in letters I can't make head nor tail of. Queer, queer stuff, I remember. Occult. Black magic.

Billy turns the page.

'Euuh!'

There's a picture ay the same wummin, but there's a boay in a long robe plungin' her wi' a blade.

'Put it doon,' I says, and take the book aff him.

But it's no' just books that's on the shelves. There's aw sorts o' spooky-lookin' gear. Wee wooden statues: women wi' big diddies, men wi' big boabbies. Normally we'd be pishin' oorsels at these, but there's somethin' giein' us the chills aboot this whole shebang. There's masks as well, some wooden efforts, but others in porcelain or plaster maybe: life-like faces, but solemn, grim even. I realise they're death masks, but don't say anythin' tae Billy.

'These must be thon arty hingmies the sergeant warned us aboot,' Billy says.

'Artefacts. Aye. I'm happy tae gie them a bodyswerve. Let's check the desk and that'll dae us.'

'Sure.'

We try the drawers on one side. They're locked, and we've no' brought anythin' tae jemmy them open.

'Forget it,' I say, hardly able tae take my eyes aff thae death masks, but Billy gie's the rest ay the drawers a pull just for the sake ay it. The bottom yin rolls open, a big, deep, heavy thing.

'Aw, man,' Billy says.

The drawer contains a glass case, and inside ay it is a skull, restin' on a bed ay velvet.

'Dae ye think it's real?' Billy asks.

'Oh Christ, aye,' I says. I've never seen a real skull, except in photies, so I wouldnae know, but I'd put money on it aw the same. I feel weird: it's giein' me the chills but I'm drawn tae it at the same time. I want tae touch it. I put my hands in and pull at the glass cover, which lifts aff nae bother.

'We cannae take it, Rab,' Billy says. 'Mind whit the Sergeant tell't us.'

'I just want tae haud it,' I tell him. I reach in and take haud ay it carefully with both hands, but it doesnae lift away. It's like it's connected tae somethin' underneath, but I can tell there's some give in it, so I try giein' it a wee twist. It turns aboot ninety degrees courtesy of a flick o' the wrist, at which point the pair ay us nearly hit the ceilin', 'cause there's a grindin' noise at oor backs and we turn roon tae see the back ay the fireplace rolled away.

'It's a secret passage,' Billy says. 'I read aboot these. Big auld hooses hud them frae back in the times when they might get invaded.'

I look into the passage, expecting darkness, but see a flickerin' light, dancin' aboot like it must be comin' fae a fire. Me and Billy look at each other. We baith know we're shitin' oorsels, but we baith know there's no way we're no' checkin' oot whatever's doon this passage.

We leave the candles because there's just aboot enough light, and we don't want tae gie oorsels away too soon if it turns oot there's somebody doon there. I go first. I duck doon tae get under the mantelpiece, but the passage is big enough for us tae staun upright once I'm on the other side. It only goes three or four yards, then there's a staircase, a tight spiral number. I haud on tae the walls as I go doon, so's my footsteps are light and quiet. I stop haufway doon and put a hand oot tae stop Billy an' aw, because we can hear a voice. It's a man talkin', except it's almost like he's singin', like a priest giein' it that high-and-mighty patter. Then we hear that sound again, and Billy was right: it is loads ay people aw at once, chantin' a reply tae whatever the man's said.

Queer, queer stuff, I'm thinkin'. Occult. Black magic.

Still, I find masel creepin' doon the rest ay the stairs. I move slow as death as I get to the bottom, and crouch in close tae the wall tae stay oot ay sight. Naebody sees us, 'cause they're aw facin' forwards away fae us in this long underground hall, kinda like a chapel but wi' nae windaes. It's lit wi' burnin' torches alang baith walls and there's a stone altar at the far end, wi' wan o' yon pentagrams painted on the wall behind it. There's aboot two dozen folk, aw wearin' these big black hooded robes, except for two ay them at the altar: the bloke that's giein' it the priest patter, who's in red, and a lassie, no' much aulder than us, in white, wi' a gag roon her mooth. She looks totally oot ay it. Billy crouches doon next tae me. We don't look at each other 'cause we cannae take oor eyes aff whit's happenin' in front ae us.

The boy in the red robe, who must be the magician that owns the joint, gie's a nod, and two of the congregation come forward and lift the lassie. It's only when they dae this that I can see her hands are tied behind her back and her feet tied at the ankles. They lay her doon on the altar and then drape a big white sheet over her, coverin' her frae heid tae toe. Then the boy in red starts chantin' again and pulls this ginormous dagger oot frae his robe. He hauds it above his heid, and everythin' goes totally still, totally quiet. Ye can hear the cracklin' ay the flames aw roon the hall. Then the congregation come oot wi' that rumblin' chant again, and he plunges the dagger doon intae the sheet.

There's mair silence, and I feel like time's staunin' still for a moment; like, when it starts again this'll no' be true. Then I see the red startin' tae seep across the white sheet, and a second later it's drippin' aff the altar ontae the flair.

'Aw Jesus,' I says. I hears masel sayin' it afore I know whit I'm daein', an' by that time it's too late.

Me and Billy turns and scrambles back up the stair as fast as, but when we get tae the top, it's just solid black-ness. The fireplace has closed over again. We see the orange flickerin' ay torches and hear footsteps comin' up the stairs. The two ay us slumped doon against a wall, haudin' on tae each other. Two men approach, then stop a few feet away, which is when wan ay them pulls his hood back.

'Evening, boys. We've been expecting you,' he says. The fuckin' Sergeant. 'I assume you took steps to make sure nobody knew where you were going tonight,' he goes on. I remember the train, the guard, the bikes, the return ticket in my trooser pocket. The Sergeant smiles. 'Knew you wouldn't let us down. What's bred in the bone, will not out of the flesh.'

Four more blokes come up tae lend a hand. They tie oor hauns and feet, same as the lassie, and huckle us back doon the stair tae the hall.

'Two more sacrifices, Master,' the Sergeant shouts oot tae the boy in red. 'As promised.'

'Are they virgins?' the Master says.

'Come on. Would anybody shag this pair?'

The master laughs and says: 'Bring them forward.'

We get carried, lyin' on oor backs, by two guys each, and it's as we pass down the centre of the hall that we see the faces peerin' in. It's aw folk fae the village. Folk we know, folk we've stolen from. I think aboot ma uncle and his blethers aboot secret gatherings. Auld bastard never knew the hauf ay it.

'This one first,' the Master says, and they lie me doon on the altar, which is still damp wi' blood. I feel it soakin' intae ma troosers as the boy starts chantin' again and a fresh white sheet comes doon tae cover me.

I don't know whether there was ether on it, or

choloroform, or maybe it was just fear, but that was the last thing I saw, 'cause I passed oot aboot two seconds later.

So.

Ye don't need many brains tae work oot what happened next, dae ye? Aye, a lesson was taught. A wise and skilled man, that magician, for he was the man in charge, the village in his thrall, willingly daein' what he told them.

Suffice it to say, we was two wee scrotes who never broke intae another hoose, and the same'll be true of you, pal.

I can see fae that look in your eye that you're sceptical aboot this. Maybe you don't believe you're no' gaunny reoffend. Nae changin' your nature, eh? What's bred in the bone, will not out of the flesh. Or maybe you don't believe my story?

Aye, that's a fair shout. I didnae tell the whole truth. The story's nae lie, but I changed the perspective a wee bit, for dramatic effect. You see, if you werenae so bliss-fully oblivious of whose hoose you happen tae be screwin' on any given night, you might have noticed fae the door-plate that my name's no Rab. I wasnae wan ay the burglars.

I was the Sergeant.

I'm retired noo, obviously, but I still perform certain services in the village. We're a close-knit community, ye could say. So I ought to let you know, when you heard me on the phone earlier, sayin' I'd caught a burglar and tae come roon soon as, it wasnae 999 I dialled. Mair like 666, if you catch my drift. 'Cause, let's face it, naebody knows you're here, dae they?

Are you a virgin, by the way?

Aye, right.

Doesnae matter really. Either way, you're well fucked noo.

Aye, good evening officer, thanks for coming. He's through there. Sorry aboot the whiff. I think you could call that the smell of restorative justice.

Go easy on him. I've a strong feelin' he's aboot tae change his ways. How do I know? Personal experience, officer. Personal experience.

ZAPRUDER
GJ Moffat

'*Back and to the left*,' the man on the TV screen says.

Freeze frame. A crimson cloud.

Play.

'*Back and to the left*.'

On the screen – panic. The woman comes out of her seat and reaches back, back. Trying desperately to reach something that skitters away across the immaculate paint of the open-topped car.

Does she realise, he wonders as he watches the film, that it's a piece of her husband's skull? His head destroyed by that final, awful bullet and she's trying to reach a bit of bone to . . . what? Press his brains back in to his head and close up the wound?

'There now,' she'll say, kissing his newly whole head. 'All better.'

No harm done.

Jackie O. No longer Jackie K. Does anyone even remember her as Jackie Kennedy? he wonders.

Then Kevin Costner comes back on screen with his artificially grey hair, his glasses and that Southern accent.

He presses STOP and the gentle hum of the DVD player winds down until it falls silent. He goes over to the machine, presses OPEN and puts the silver disc carefully back in its case, running his fingers over the raised lettering on the front cover: *JFK*.

'I remember where I was,' he says aloud, his eyes glistening wetly in the dark of the room. 'I remember hope.'

He feels the tears there; brimming and ready to spill

out, but tries so hard not to squeeze his eyes shut and force them out. Because he fears what he'll see when the shutters come down; what he always sees.

But he does anyway; he closes his eyes.

His breath hitches in his chest and he sees her again, his wife . . .

Back and to the left.

. . . her head snapping back as they kick her over and over and over, two of them pinning his arms behind his back. She eventually stops making a sound. Stops breathing. And he tells them again as they turn to him, *we have no money here, there's nothing I can do about it.*

But they don't stop; they never do. Sallow skin, drawn and unnatural in pallor. Eyes hooded from the drugs or alcohol coursing through their blood.

Her blood is on the carpet, seeping and staining. Underneath, the floorboards permanently marked with her life essence. All that's left of her now.

'Maria,' he says, his voice broken and cracked.

It's all that he can say before the tears take over and then he's bent double sobbing; his mouth open in a silent scream.

PTSD, that's what they call it.

All of them. The counsellor and the Victim Support officer and his daughter, Jane.

Post-Traumatic Stress Disorder.

'It's why you keep seeing it, Dad,' Jane told him. 'Like

a film running in your head every time you close your eyes.'

'I know,' he replied dully. 'The doctor told me already.'

'You need to talk about it with the counsellor, Dad.'

Arm around his shoulder, sitting next to him on the couch.

'He said that as well.'

She sighed beside him and leaned her head in till it rested against his.

He remembered something else then, something to ease the pain and hold back the rolling black waves of fear. Holding Jane as a baby, her head lolling on his shoulder, her neck muscles still too weak to support her own head. The smell of breast milk on her breath and powder on her skin.

It should be a more powerful memory. It's not fair. Life is more powerful than death so why is it that every time he closes his eyes all he sees is Jane's mother.

Dying.

Why did she have to be the one that answered the door to them? Why couldn't it have been him?

Survivor guilt: they've got a name for everything.

'You can't blame yourself, Dad.' Jane again, always the comforter.

He's noticed that she does that now when she speaks to him. Calls him 'Dad' at the end of every sentence.

'Cup of tea, Dad?'

'Shall I pick up some milk for you, Dad?'

'Need anything, Dad?'

She's trying to be strong for him, he knows. But he resents her for it. He's her father, after all. It's the parents that are supposed to look after the children, not the other way around.

He hates it; getting old. Being old. Nothing works like it used to. Nothing looks the way it used to look.

Never used to hate it. Not until . . .

As a man he was always comfortable in his own skin, enjoying each age and the new experiences the new era brought. Mostly it was Jane, seeing her grow. First as a baby that he held in his arms, then soon, far too soon, as an adult off living her own life. Where did all the time go? And now she was soon-to-be-mother Jane. Her bump getting bigger by the day it seemed to him.

That was how the night had started; the night they came. With the bump.

It was a hot July day and Maria had called him in from the garden when Jane came over. Sitting together in the kitchen, Jane squirming and laughing as the baby inside kicked out at her.

He had reached over and placed his hand on her stomach, feeling tiny fists and feet swirl around inside.

'He'll be just like you, Jane,' Maria said. 'I mean, you could never stay still. I think if they'd been able to see inside me I'd have been black and blue.'

They laughed.

He stayed crouched in front of his daughter and rested

his head on her belly, hearing the gurgles and sloshes of the baby, feeling a gentle kick against his head.

'He was never this soppy when I was pregnant with you,' Maria said, nudging him in the side with her knee.

'Different times,' he said, standing.

He turned to his wife. On the last day of her life. Put his arms around her waist and kissed her on the cheek.

Their last kiss.

Back and to the left.

The gun was well cared for, he had always seen to that.

Georg J Luger had given his name to a weapon that was, in equal parts, beautiful and terrible.

His father had brought it back from the War. He had been eight when his father sat him down and unwrapped the oil-stained cloth to show him his spoils.

'You know where I've been, son?' his father asked.

'Away.'

Lines creased his father's face as he smiled. He remembered thinking then that he looked older than he should. He was only twenty-four when he came back from the War but it had aged him ten years or more.

'Away is right. Far away. But I'm back now and I'll not be going away again.'

He recalled the heavy sound of the gun, still wrapped in the cloth, when his father took it from his kit bag and placed it on the table. His mother stood behind them, watching with a frown on her face but saying nothing.

'Do you know what a gun is, Jimmy?' his father asked.

'Like Cowboys and Indians?'

'Just like that, yes.'

'And do you know what it can do?'

'Kill people?'

'That's right.'

That's when he started to peel the cloth back – always a sense of drama with him. When he was done and the weapon was exposed, it looked ordinary and unremarkable.

'It's a beauty, eh, son?'

He didn't know how to respond. Didn't want to say that, no, it didn't look like much at all to him.

'Did you kill someone to get it?' was what he finally said.

'No, son, but somebody did. Jerry deserved all that he got and don't let anyone tell you any different.' Winking at his mother and her tutting.

The boy, him, still staring, and slowly becoming entranced by the dark majesty of the thing on the table.

Now, though, it was nothing more than a family heirloom. He kept it oiled and stored away safely, only taking it down occasionally to run his hand over it and grip the handle. Remembering his father now many years passed. His strongest memory of the man and still his greatest connection to him.

On this day, his last he has decided, he goes to the wardrobe and pulls the box down. Carries it down the stairs and into the kitchen. He imagines that he smells Maria's gingerbread, baking in the oven and releasing those spices into the air. Best to eat it hot with some proper butter melting on top and a cup of strong, milky tea on the side.

He sits at the table and is about to close his eyes; one last test, to see if those images are still there. The ones he wants to blow out of his skull for good.

Back and to the left.

There will be no Jackie O to scamper after his skull. No one to put him together again.

The phone rings in the front room. He doesn't want to answer it because people always talk to him the same way now – careful. He hates careful. Wants to shout at all of them that what he needs is his old life back, when they spoke to him like a normal person. About normal things.

The football.

The weather.

EastEnders (which he hates).

It rings and it rings and then it stops.

He waits, his hand resting on top of the box with Georg's creation sitting inside. He hears it whisper to him and its voice is harsh and metallic.

Take me, it whispers.

Touch me.

Use me.

'I will,' he tells it.

And when he closes his eyes he sees it all again, presses

his hands to his head and tries to squeeze the memories out of there.

Back and to the left.

The phone rings again.

And then again.

They're worried about him, no doubt. He missed his counselling this week and that always sends up the red flag. Didn't speak much when the Victim Support woman was over for her tea and biscuits. Had to make up some excuse about having a cold when he spoke with Jane.

'You're getting worse, Dad,' she told him. 'Let me find a different doctor for you. A private one. We'll pay for it, Robert and me.'

Ring-ring.

Ring-ring.

Ring-ring.

He goes through to the hall and pulls the phone jack out of the socket. No more interruptions.

He needs to get on with the job at hand.

Back in the kitchen he fidgets for a while. A cup of tea and then another. He finally sits down at the table and takes great care in opening the box and removing the gun from the cloth, the same oil-stained cloth. It's almost ceremonial. It should be; the import of what is about to be done demands it.

There are three bullets for it, he knows. He hopes that at least one of them still works. He realises a little too late that perhaps he should have checked; he's not sure if sixty-year-old rounds will still work.

He wastes no time. He lifts a bullet, loads the gun, puts it against his temple and pulls the trigger.

Click.

Some sixty-year-old rounds don't work.

'No,' he says, softly.

He realises that it'll never be that easy to do again. The first time is the best because you have no concept of what will happen.

Click.

Click.

He takes the bullet out and replaces it with another. Only one more after this one and then what will he do? Best not to think about it.

The doorbell sounds. It's an old house and still has the original bell. It doesn't work perfectly every time so there's a hesitant quality to it.

He waits, placing the gun on the table and rubbing his hands on his thighs, unaware of the sweat soaking into his trousers. The bell rings again. He gets up and walks to the hall, seeing a shadow behind the frosted doorpane.

The shadow rings the bell twice more and then starts to talk to itself. Then he realises that it's talking to someone on a mobile phone. He leaves the shadow to its business and walks back to the kitchen.

The gun looks different now. Bigger. He picks it up. It

feels heavier. Lets it drop back onto the table, still with his fingers wrapped around it.

'Give me the strength to do this, Maria,' he says. 'Let me be with you.'

And he tries to push away the image that comes into his head, of Maria waiting to greet him with her arms outstretched. But something about her doesn't look right and as he draws near he sees what it is. Her face is misshapen, as though the attack has just happened. Blood pulses down and soaks her clothes.

He shakes his head and smacks his hands against his face. He needs to be rid of this. He can't live like this any longer.

He lifts the gun to his head again and squeezes.

Click.

Click.

Click-click-click-click-click.

He drops the gun and lays his head on the table.

'Why?' he says. 'Why can't I do this? Let me have peace.'

He's never been religious and is not entirely sure whom he's talking to. It just seems like there must be someone.

Anyone.

The doorbell rings again.

Then he hears the letterbox opening.

'Mister Shepherd!' the shadow shouts. 'Are you all right?'

It's the woman from Victim Support. He holds his breath, as if somehow that makes him invisible, like he never lived here.

Please, go away.

'Mister Shepherd!'

He reaches out and reloads. The final bullet. Last chance.

Please work this time.

Touches the barrel of the gun to his head, feels the caress of the cold metal.

His last kiss.

Puts his finger on the trigger.

The letterbox opens again.

Applies pressure to the trigger.

A bit more.

Sees Maria again, this time as she was on their wedding day – always smiling, dancing while everyone applauded. The first dance.

Back and to the left.

Her last dance – not with him. With them.

He applies more pressure.

Hears the shadow shout through the letterbox, though she sounds different now.

Let me go.

It's not the shadow, he realises.

His finger eases the trigger back, waiting for the firing mechanism to activate and release him from the pain. Blessed relief.

It's Jane.

His Jane.

'Dad, it's me. Dad, please answer me.'

Her voice is different.

'Dad, answer me.'

She's crying.

Baby Jane.

Maria's milk sour/sweet on her breath. Their blood in hers. Hers in the new life inside her.

'Dad!' Screaming. '*Daaaaad!*'

He jerks his head, desperately trying to pull away from the coming fire. Too late, is it too late now?

The trigger finally clicks all the way back.

The bullet is live. It explodes from the gun and roars past his forehead as he pulls away from it, cracking out of the kitchen window, shattering the glass as it goes.

Jane screams.

He drops the gun.

He stands on unsteady legs and stumbles towards the sound of his daughter's tears, towards his grandson.

Towards life.

WRITERS' BIOGRAPHIES

LIN ANDERSON

Lin Anderson is a graduate of Glasgow and Edinburgh Universities and was recently awarded an MA Screenwriting with Distinction from the Screen Academy Scotland. Her short film *River Child* won a student BAFTA and the Celtic Film Festival best fiction award. She has published five novels in her crime series featuring Glasgow-based forensic scientist Rhona MacLeod which have been translated into a number of languages. The sixth, *Final Cut*, is published on 6 August 2009 and is being developed as a three-parter for ITV. Her website is www.lin-anderson.com.

RAY BANKS

Ray Banks is the author of five novels, four featuring his private eye Callum Innes (the most recent being *Beast of Burden*), as well as a clutch of short stories and a novella for Crime Express called *Gun*. He lives in Newcastle-upon-Tyne, but is mostly found at his website: www.thesaturdayboy.com.

CHRISTOPHER BROOKMYRE

Christopher Brookmyre's first novel, *Quite Ugly One Morning*, was published in 1996 and won the First Blood Award for Best First Crime Novel of the Year. Since then he has published twelve further novels, the latest of which is *Pandaemonium*. In 2006 he won the PG Wodehouse Prize for *All Fun and Games until Somebody Loses an Eye*, and in 2007 he was given the Glenfiddich Spirit of Scotland Award for Writing. However, he is a St Mirren season-ticket holder, so it's not all a success story. His website is www.brookmyre. co.uk.

KAREN CAMPBELL

A former police officer, Karen Campbell is also a graduate of Glasgow University's Creative Writing Masters. She is the author of *The Twilight Time* (Hodder 2008) and *After the Fire* (Hodder 2009), and was voted Best New Scottish Writer at the 2009 Scottish Variety Awards. Her website is www.karencampbell.co.uk.

GILLIAN GALBRAITH

Gillian Galbraith practised as an Advocate at the Scottish Bar for many years. She is the author of *Blood in the Water*, *Where the Shadow Falls* and *Dying of the Light*. She lives in the country with her husband and daughter plus assorted dogs, cats, bees and goats.

ALEX GRAY

Alex Gray was born and educated in Glasgow, the city that provides the backdrop to her DCI Lorimer crime novels. After studying English at the University of Strathclyde, her postgraduate education was working as a DSS officer in Old Govan. Memories of Wine Alley and its inhabitants possibly lingered in her subconscious, being dredged up as material for fictional characters. Alex thoroughly enjoys her life of crime, knowing that she can bump off anyone she likes with impunity, even killing off a controversial football referee in one book. Yet folk who know her claim she's a nice lady, really. Her website is www.alex-gray.com.

ALLAN GUTHRIE

Allan Guthrie is a crime writer and literary agent who lives in Edinburgh. His latest novel is *Slammer*. His website is www.allanguthrie.co.uk.

STUART MACBRIDE

Stuart MacBride has gone from asking people if they 'want fries with that' to project managing vast IT projects for the oil industry. He's the bestselling author of gruesome crime novels set in Aberdeen: *Cold Granite*, *Dying Light*, *Broken Skin*, *Flesh House* and *Blind Eye*; a near future thriller called *Halfhead*; and *Sawbones*, a short and nasty novella for reluctant readers.

To everyone's surprise, Stuart won the CWA's Dagger in the Library in 2007, a Barry in 2005, the ITV3 Breakthrough Award in 2008, and has been shortlisted for a bunch of other stuff.

He also has a beard.

His website is www.stuartmacbride.com.

GJ MOFFAT

GJ Moffat is a father, husband, writer and lawyer though sometimes he's not quite sure in what order. He always had the urge to write about good guys and bad guys, and his debut novel *Daisychain* brings them to life in glorious Technicolor. His second novel *Fallout* will be published in early 2010. He is married with two little angel girls and is struggling to learn the electric guitar (hitting more bum notes than good ones).

IAN RANKIN

Ian Rankin is the creator of Inspector Rebus. The books have been international bestsellers and are translated into thirty-two languages. His website is www.ianrankin.net.

LOUISE WELSH

Louise Welsh is the author of three novels, *The Cutting Room*, *Tamburlaine Must Die* and *The Bullet Trick*, all published by Canongate Books. Her fourth novel, *Naming the Bones*, will hit the shelves in March 2010. Louise lives in Glasgow.

VICTIM SUPPORT SCOTLAND

Many people will be affected by crime at some point in their life, either directly as a victim or witness – maybe just by being in the wrong place at the wrong time – or indirectly through family, friends or work colleagues. The physical, psychological and emotional effects can be devastating.

From its modest beginnings in Coatbridge in the 1980s, Victim Support Scotland (VSS) has helped more than one million people, providing emotional support, practical help and information, as well as being instrumental in raising the profile of victims and witnesses in the public, parliamentary and criminal justice arenas.

Last year the charity helped 160,000 people affected by crime; within a few years the number is likely to surpass 200,000. The charity is recognised throughout Europe as one of the most effective organisations in the field of victim support.

While our work has been much praised by the Scottish Government and we are indebted to our President, HRH The Princess Royal, the level of funding we receive limits our ability to develop as we would like. Therefore, the support of all the contributors to this book in donating their royalties, and Birlinn Ltd in assisting with the project and its launch, is a tremendous gesture.

If you wish to find out more about our activities,

including the Witness Service and Youth Justice Service, or make a donation supporting our work you can do so securely via our website.

Scottish Helpline: 0845 603 9213
Website: www.victimsupportsco.org.uk

ACKNOWLEDGEMENTS

Thanks go to: Neville Moir at Birlinn for seeing the potential of this project; Alison Rae at Polygon for being a great editor; fundraiser Maureen McKellar who came up with the original idea for the collection; and all the writers who supported this project from the outset and contributed fantastic stories.